"Alex relies on her powers too much!" Annie said.

"I do not!" Alex shot back.

"You do, too!" Her sister looked over at her. "Why didn't you just get the spare key? Why did you have to morph?"

"Is that why you're so mad at me, Annie? Because I can do things you can't?"

"Give me a break! I'm *upset* because you're using your powers in public. You're forgetting how to think!"

"I am not!" Alex insisted stubbornly.

"You couldn't get through one day without using your powers for something."

"Could, too!"

"Then prove it. I dare you to go twenty-four hours without using your powers."

"You're on!" Alex said without hesitation. *How hard could it be?* she wondered. Then she noticed her sister's smug smile....

The Secret World of Alex Mack™

Alex, You're Glowing!
Bet You Can't!

Available from MINSTREL Books

NICKELODEON™

the secret world of

ALEX MACK™

Bet You Can't!

Diana G. Gallagher

A MINSTREL® BOOK

PUBLISHED BY POCKET BOOKS

New York   London   Toronto   Sydney   Tokyo   Singapore

A MINSTREL PAPERBACK *Original*

A Minstrel Book published by
POCKET BOOKS, a division of Simon & Schuster Inc.
1230 Avenue of the Americas, New York, NY 10020

ISBN: 0-671-53300-2

First Minstrel Books printing June 1995

10 9 8 7 6 5 4 3 2 1

Printed in the U.S.A.

For Kelley Judd
an enthusiastic and helpful friend

CHAPTER 1

Alex Mack lagged behind her mother and sister as they marched through the aisles of the large department store. It was just after five o'clock on Friday evening, and Paradise Valley Mall was already crowded. But the throngs of shoppers surrounding her didn't prevent Alex from spying a rack of quilted vests with gorgeous buttons. She stopped and ran her hand over the soft velvet, then checked the price tag. *Maybe it will go on sale soon,* she thought. *I could wear it with my—*

"Move it, Alex!" her sister, Annie, demanded with an impatient glance backward.

Alex dropped the price tag and ran to catch up with her mom and Annie. Her mother had been talking about having a yard sale for months. She had finally decided to do it this weekend, and she wanted to buy their supplies and leave the mall as soon as possible. There was a lot to do before they set up shop on the front lawn in the morning.

"The more signs we put up, the more people we'll get," Annie said as Alex fell into step behind them.

"Very good, Annie." Mrs. Mack grinned at her oldest daughter. Barbara Mack was a successful account executive at a local public relations firm as well as a dedicated wife and mother. Annie was a scientific genius, like Mr. Mack, and rarely took more than a casual interest in her mother's business.

"You can't sell anything unless the public knows you have something to sell," Mrs. Mack said, delighted by Annie's enthusiasm. "Public Relations one-oh-one."

Alex stopped to look at a display of color-coordinated soaps and lotions wrapped three to a basket. She had never been interested in pretty toiletries before, but suddenly the feminine scents and bottles attracted her. *Maybe because I really am starting to grow up. . . .*

As Alex turned, a small boy dashed past, deliberately hitting the stack of baskets with his hand. Laughing, he bolted down an aisle to the right, his untied shoelace flapping as he ran. The carefully arranged baskets began to fall. The ones on the bottom went first, upsetting the balance of the baskets on top of the pile.

Uh-oh, avalanche, Alex thought. Automatically she concentrated intensely on the tumbling display. The falling baskets stopped in midair, then slowly slid back into place on the shelf.

"Alex!" Annie hissed a warning.

Alex gasped, realizing what she had done. Ever since she'd almost been run down by a Paradise Valley Chemical truck and accidentally doused with the mysterious chemical GC 161, she'd had a big secret to keep. The golden gunk had drenched her from head to toe, and besides totally grossing her out, it had produced some really bizarre side effects. Like the ability she had just used to keep the baskets from falling. Her sister the brain called it telekinetic power. She always had a fancy name for everything. Alex could also shoot electrical charges from her fingers. Her sister called it reversal of energy fields, or something equally boring. Alex called it zapping. And Alex could even turn into a puddle of clear gel and ooze herself anywhere she wanted to go—even into tiny places like keyholes. Her sister called it metamorphosing, but Alex just called it morphing. Her best friend and next-door neighbor, Raymond Alvarado, called it radical. He was the only person besides Annie who knew her secret.

And he was the only person who could ever know. Even her close friends, Robyn and Nicole, had no idea. Most important, the suits over at Paradise Valley Chemical could never, ever find out. Danielle Atron, chief executive officer of the plant, had developed the illegal gene-altering chemical, which she hoped someday would enable people to do things like pig out all day and never gain a pound, even if they never hauled their butts off the couch once in their life. GC 161 was still in the experimental stage. Annie figured this out when she saw that it made Alex glow a strange gold color whenever she got too excited or embarrassed. "It must be experimental," she'd explained to Alex. "No one would actually want to walk around looking like an extraterrestrial."

So Danielle Atron and her security guy, Vince,

were determined to find the kid who'd been doused by the nasty goo. The guy driving the GC 161 in a truck had never gotten a good look at Alex, and it was important that they find her before she went to the authorities. But Annie decided the best thing to do would be to keep quiet. If anyone found out, the plant could close down, and her father, a chemist employed there, could lose his job. Plus, Annie saw it as a great opportunity to research the experimental compound, which probably hadn't yet been tested, even on animals. "In other words," she'd told her sister, "you're a perfect stand-in for a laboratory rat."

Alex quickly looked around the store. What if someone had seen her move the baskets? The shoppers were all intent on finding the bargain of the century, and no one seemed to have noticed Alex or her magic powers. Relieved, Alex countered Annie's glare with a satisfied smile. She knew Annie was only concerned for her safety, but sometimes Alex wished she'd lighten up a little.

"Alex, we're in a hurry," Mrs. Mack said as she moved on into women's accessories.

"Now, Alex." Exasperated, Annie turned and stalked away.

"Annie, do I need to remind you that I already have a mother?" Alex said to Annie's back. "You're the sister, remember? Only two years older than me. . . ." But she didn't say it loud enough for Annie to hear, and instead she played it safe, dawdling near a display of hats around a mirror.

Lacking the brilliant aptitude for science and math Annie shared with their father, or the dramatic flair and style of their mother, Alex felt painfully average. She was not average anymore, of course, thanks to the side effects of GC 161. But since no one knew about her powers except Annie and Raymond, she was still plain, old Alex Mack to everyone else.

Slim with long, straight, dark blond hair and large brown eyes, Alex was convinced she even looked hopelessly average . . . except for her hats.

She had begun adding to her collection of baseball caps shortly after the GC 161 accident. Hats of various colors and styles had taken over the top shelf of the bedroom closet she shared with Annie. The more outrageous the hat, the better. They had become Alex's silent statement to the world that said, "This is who I am," she was different, and she didn't care who laughed at her bizarre sense of fashion.

She flipped a black velvet hat onto her head, then looked into the small mirror. The front edge of the wide brim was turned up and fastened to the crown by a cluster of artificial, shocking pink roses surrounded by iridescent green leaves. She was turning the hat to see how it would look sideways when a sudden, sharp pain shot through her foot.

"Ow!" Alex squealed in surprise. With a grimace she looked down to see a thick-soled Doc Marten crushing her foot, which was protected only by a canvas tennis shoe.

"Oh, I'm so sorry," a girl's voice said sincerely. "Did I hurt you?"

Alex was trying to decide whether or not to answer the question honestly when she realized, with a slight shock, that she recognized the girl who had trampled on her. It was Rhonda Clark, the coolest, most totally perfect girl in seventh grade. With long curly blond hair and huge blue eyes, Rhonda looked like a model out of *Seventeen*. "Not exactly a bowser," as Raymond put it. Rhonda was also a straight-A student, captain of the seventh-grade debate team, and star of the next school play. Rhonda and her select friends kept to themselves most of the time. Alex had never spoken to her before, and she didn't know quite what to say now, though she decided that answering the question honestly was *not* the thing to do.

"Uh—hi, Rhonda."

"Oh, hi, I didn't recognize you under that hat. You're Alexandra Mack, right? I'm sorry I stepped on your foot," Rhonda said.

She knows my *name?* Alex thought to herself.

"I guess I was too busy checking out the hats and everything, and I didn't even see you," Rhonda went on. "Anyway, that hat looks really cool. It's definitely you."

"You think so?' Alex said, surprised.

"Totally," Rhonda said. "You can wear hats. I never could. I always feel silly in them, like I'm playing dress-up with my mother's clothes or something." Rhonda picked up a straw hat with a sunflower tucked in the band and tried it on. She looked in the mirror, made a disgusted face, and threw the hat back in the pile.

"Here, try this one," Alex said, handing her a suede baseball cap. "It'll look good with your hair."

Rhonda tried the hat on, looked in the mirror, and shrugged. "I don't think it's my best look," she said and took the hat off.

Alex thought the hat looked perfect on Rhonda and said so. But Rhonda just shrugged and shook her hair back into place.

"Well, I'd better go. Guess I'll see you in school sometime," Rhonda said with a little wave.

"Uh—okay," was all Alex could manage.

"Sorry about your foot," Rhonda called back.

"No problem," Alex said. She couldn't believe how nice Rhonda was. She never thought someone like Rhonda would ever notice her, let alone know her name. And Rhonda had even said she'd see her in school sometime! Alex looked in the mirror and smiled at her reflection. *Maybe this hat really is me*, she thought.

"Alex! Let's go!" Mrs. Mack said sharply, rushing to Alex's side. "Maybe you should have waited in the car."

Alex tried not to blush. Rhonda had stopped by the jewelry counter only a few feet away and could have heard everything her mother just said. Alex wanted to hide, she was so embarrassed. All she needed was to start glowing in front everyone at the mall.

"That hat *is* adorable, honey," Mrs. Mack said in a softer tone. "But we're running out of time."

"Yeah, I know," Alex said. "Sorry."

"Lose the hat, Alex," Annie said.

"I like it," Alex snapped defiantly, glancing over at Rhonda.

Annie's taste was a little more conservative. "But, Alex, it clashes with everything you own, and it probably glows in the dark. Come to think of it, it *is* you."

"Enough, Annie," Mrs. Mack said sternly. "We really do have to get going, Alex. It's going to take a while to make all those signs and put them up around the neighborhood, even with both of you working on it. No time for hats now."

"You go on, Mom. I'll catch up in a minute." Alex just couldn't bring herself to leave with her mother and sister, looking like a little kid in tow. Rhonda was still nearby.

"Don't get lost." When Mrs. Mack planted a kiss on Alex's forehead, Alex mumbled, "Gee Mom, I've never been to a mall before." Barbara Mack just smiled and headed toward the entrance to the mall. Annie went with her.

Noting that Rhonda had moved on, Alex looked in the mirror again. Maybe Annie was right. Did the black velvet hat with shocking pink and green foliage look totally geeky with her orange-and-blue-striped T-shirt? Rhonda had liked it. Alex put the hat back on the rack and shuffled toward the jewelry counter across the aisle. A sign caught her eye and she hesitated.

EARS PIERCED FREE WITH PURCHASE
OF TWO PAIR OF EARRINGS

Maybe it's time to ditch the hats and try something new, Alex thought as she toyed with a set of dangling, silver earrings inlaid with royal-blue stones. She scanned the display, noting the variety of earwear. Feathers and beads, wood and metal, long and short, gaudy and plain . . . as Annie would say, a design to fit every mood of a thirteen-year-old girl in the grip of a constant identity crisis.

Besides, she thought, *earrings don't take up nearly as much room as hats, which will certainly please Annie the neat freak.* Annie complained at least three times a day about the mess in the closet they shared. And Alex knew her mother wouldn't care if she decided to punch holes in her ears. Most of the girls in the seventh grade at Danielle Atron Junior High had pierced ears. It was the idea of actually punching her earlobes that gave Alex the shivers. Nicole said they used a gun, which gave Alex visions of pistols and bullets. Since she didn't know how ear-piercing was done exactly, she decided to ask.

"Hello?" Alex called in the general direction of the jewelry counter. Nobody answered. Leaning across the glass case, she called again, but the jewelry department seemed to be unattended at the moment.

Having made up her mind to investigate the primitive process of ear-piercing, Alex began to search the immediate area. She wandered back through hats and handbags, past belts and scarves and into socks, but she couldn't find a salesclerk anywhere.

Knowing that Annie and her mother would return to her last known location after they had found their yard-sale supplies, Alex decided to wait at the jewelry counter. Someone had to show up eventually, and she could pass the time deciding which two pair of earrings most suited the image she wanted to project. She picked up a pair of small gold hoops and held them to her ear as she looked in a mirror on the counter. Nah. To small and safe and ordinary. They screamed,

"Alex Mack is a hopelessly average teenager with absolutely no imagination or originality."

Next she held up a pair of big gold hoops, almost as big as a bracelet, with hand-painted beads attached. Much better, she thought. They said, "Alex Mack is an incredibly talented human who not only can transform herself into a puddle of Jell-O and move things effortlessly with her mind, but also knows how to accessorize her outfits exquisitely."

Admiring the earrings in the mirror, Alex was surprised to see Rhonda pass by behind her. The other girl hadn't noticed Alex, who suddenly wondered if the large hoops were so exquisite after all. She put the earrings back on the rack.

Maybe Rhonda has pierced ears and won't mind answering some intelligent questions, Alex mused. Starting a casual conversation about something as cool as pierced ears was the perfect way to get friendly with Rhonda.

Rhonda stopped at the next counter down. Starting around the high, swivel racks of bracelets and necklaces, Alex moved toward Rhonda, then froze.

Rhonda looked right and left, then dropped an earring card into her jacket pocket. She paused to glance at an assortment of phony antique cameos, then calmly walked away.

Alex couldn't believe what her eyes had just seen. Her heart took a major jolt, and she felt the familiar tingling that told her she might soon start glowing.

Could it be true? Rhonda was shoplifting?

CHAPTER 2

Why would a girl as smart and popular as Rhonda want to steal a pair of earrings she could afford to buy? Both her parents worked in high-level positions at Paradise Valley Chemical, so Alex knew money wasn't a problem.

It just didn't make sense.

Bewildered, Alex followed the girl into the junior sportswear department. Maybe Rhonda just wanted to experience the thrill of getting away with the theft. Or maybe she thought she could talk her way out of trouble if she got caught. She *was* the captain of the seventh-grade debate team, and she *would* be caught. As soon as Rhonda tried to leave the store, the security coding on the card would trigger alarms.

Shoplifting was a serious crime. *And,* Alex thought with mounting unease, *the department store might even have Rhonda arrested!*

When Rhonda stopped to browse, Alex decided to act. She just couldn't let her commit a crime and ruin her life without *trying* to stop her.

Trying to appear casual, Alex strolled forward. Sifting through a stack of sweatshirts, Rhonda didn't see her. Alex continued toward Rhonda. Turning her head so that she appeared to be absorbed with some T-shirts across the aisle, Alex deliberately nudged the girl.

Rhonda jumped and looked at Alex, her cheeks flushing.

"Rhonda! Hello again," Alex said, trying to sound surprised.

"Oh, hi there," Rhonda said. Her eyes shifted around the store, not looking directly at Alex.

What was I thinking? Alex silently scolded herself. Asking Rhonda about getting her ears pierced was one thing. Accusing her of stealing was something else entirely. *A sure way to end all hope of ever being accepted by Rhonda or her crowd, Alex!*

Another thought suddenly occurred to her. What if Rhonda intended all along to pay for the earrings? She hadn't actually left the store yet. . . .

Alex wished she had just minded her own business, but there was no turning back now. "I, umm, I wanted to ask about your ears—uh—earrings, I mean. I really like that silver pair you picked out."

"What earrings?" Rhonda said, tossing her hair over her shoulder. Alex thought she saw the girl's face grow a deeper shade of pink.

Alex hesitated. *Now what should I do? Come right out and accuse her of stealing?*

But Rhonda wasn't going to wait around to give Alex the chance. "Gotta go," she said and spun around in the direction of the exit.

Now Alex was pretty sure that Rhonda meant to walk out of the store without paying, and as soon as she did the alarm would sound. *She should know better*, Alex thought. Maybe she didn't know better. Maybe Rhonda didn't realize there was an alarm by the exit! *I have to stop her*, Alex decided. *It's the only thing to do.*

And there was only one way to do it.

Alex couldn't bring herself to openly accuse and embarrass the girl, so she decided she'd levitate the earrings out of Rhonda's pocket. First she'd have to distract her.

"Rhonda! Wait!"

Rhonda stopped, then turned impatiently. "What?"

"Does it hurt?"

"Does what hurt?"

"Having your ears pierced." Alex knew she sounded like a complete jerk, but she didn't care.

Rhonda looked at her as if she were some kind of alien life-form and shook her head in disbelief.

"Does it?" Alex persisted. "Hurt I mean. 'Cause I was thinking of having mine done and . . ." Alex had to concentrate to move things with her mind, and using her power of telekinesis while holding a humiliating conversation wasn't easy.

"Of course it hurts!" Rhonda raised her voice angrily. "They shoot a gold stud through your earlobe with a gun!"

Alex shuddered at the thought, but managed to focus on easing the card to the top of the pocket.

"Is there a problem here?"

The gruff, deep voice came from behind Alex, breaking her train of thought. The earrings fell back into Rhonda's pocket as Alex looked over her shoulder with a startled gasp. A tall, muscular security guard glared at her suspiciously.

"No, sir," Alex said quickly. "No problem."

"No problem at all," Rhonda added. The blood drained from her face, and Alex could tell she was terrified.

The man studied them steadily for a long moment, then left.

"Catch a clue, Alex, and get lost!" Rhonda said as she took off.

Alex had no choice but to let Rhonda go. The security guard might still be watching, and she didn't dare draw his attention again. If she was smart, she'd just let Rhonda get caught leaving the store with stolen goods. It would serve her right.

Mystified, Alex followed Rhonda at a discreet distance. Something about the whole situation seemed odd. Almost like Rhonda *wanted* to get caught. Why? Rhonda Clark had everything going for her. She was smart, athletic, pretty, and popular—and yet she seemed determined to destroy it all with one stupid act of petty theft.

As Rhonda approached the automatic doors, Alex realized she was acting like a spineless dork.

Rhonda had been rude and insulting, and Alex had let her get away with it! No longer caring whether Rhonda got caught or not, Alex was determined to prove that she wasn't a wimp. She would confront Rhonda and insist that she put the earrings back.

But first she had to prevent the girl from leaving and setting off the alarms between the inner and outer sets of doors.

Alex focused on the exit as Rhonda stepped onto the black mat that triggered the doors to open. The doors began to slide apart, then reversed direction and closed with a thud—only inches from Rhonda's face.

Rhonda hesitated, then pounded on the glass. Nothing happened, and she kicked the metal frame in frustration.

Alex held the doors together with the force of her mind.

Turning, Rhonda darted to the next set of doors, a few feet away. They were not automatic, and Alex wasn't sure she could hold them closed when Rhonda threw her weight against them to get out. Alex shifted her concentration to a group of metal shopping carts lined up near the doors. With her mind she sent them rolling forward.

Then she disengaged her telekinetic power and moved toward Rhonda.

The carts continued to roll under their own momentum.

Just then a tall, muscular boy and a short, stocky girl entered through the automatic doors, which were no longer being held closed by Alex's thoughts.

Alex immediately recognized Mike Warner and Meg Halsey, ninth-grade punks who got into trouble as if it were a hobby. Both were wearing torn, faded jeans, black leather jackets, and boots. Alex remembered Annie saying the high school truant officer planned to dedicate the detention room to them, with a plaque bearing their names and everything.

The carts rolled in front of Rhonda, blocking the manual doors. They kept right on rolling toward the automatic doors.

Mike and Meg jumped clear just before the carts rolled into them. A second later the carts hit the wall with a resounding crash. Meg shrieked and staggered.

The last three carts slammed into the end of the line, bounced off, and came to rest at odd angles.

Startled by the moving carts and trapped inside

the store, Rhonda whirled around in panic. She collided with Meg Halsey, knocking her off her feet.

Alex reached Rhonda's side just as Meg grabbed on to a loose shopping cart to steady herself. Instead of saving her, the cart toppled over. With another high-pitched scream, Meg crumpled to the floor underneath it.

Out of the corner of her eye Alex saw the security guard rushing toward the commotion from the men's department. In front of her Mike Warner pulled the cart off Meg with one hand and helped her up with the other.

"What d'ya think you're doin' huh?" Mike bellowed at Rhonda. "Someone could've gotten hurt!"

"I *did* get hurt!" Meg sneered.

"But I didn't do—" Rhonda tried to explain.

"Get off it! I saw you!" Mike shouted. "These shopping carts didn't start rolling by themselves, and no one else was anywhere near them!"

"Nobody but you!" Meg's broad face darkened in a scowl.

"But they *did* move by themselves!" Rhonda insisted frantically.

Still holding on to the cart that had run her

over, Meg gave it a shove and sent it barreling toward Rhonda.

Alex stopped the forward movement with a thought before the cart hit the petrified girl beside her. The cart rolled back, and Mike grabbed it before it hit him.

"I don't know how you did that, but you're messin' with the wrong guy!" Mike snarled at Rhonda.

"Did what?" Rhonda asked, puzzled and frightened.

Kicking the cart out of the way, Mike took a menacing step toward Alex and Rhonda. "You and your friend better get out of my way—"

"And you'd better get out of my store!"

Four startled faces turned to stare at the angry security guard. He stepped in front of Alex and Rhonda and glared at Mike and Meg as he pointed toward the exit.

"Out!" the man's voice boomed with authority.

"But we didn't do anything!" Meg protested loudly.

"They started it!" Mike waved toward Alex and Rhonda.

"I've seen you both in here before, making trouble. Get out! Now!" The security guard's eyes narrowed in warning.

Mike took Meg's hand and pushed through the shopping carts barricading the exit. As they stalked toward the automatic doors, the tall boy glanced back. His gaze swept over Alex and settled on Rhonda for a long moment. Then he dragged the pouting Meg outside.

"You two okay?" the guard asked.

"We're fine. Thanks," Alex said.

Rhonda nodded, then turned to leave as the guard walked away. Alex pivoted, about to try to stop Rhonda again, when out of the corner of her eye she noticed Annie, leaning against a counter. Her arms were crossed, and she was watching with an angry frown. Two large shopping bags sat on the floor beside her.

Uh-oh, Alex thought anxiously. *How much of the incident had Annie seen? Maybe worse ... what did Rhonda suspect?* Mike and Meg thought Rhonda had pushed the carts. But Rhonda knew that she hadn't touched them.

"Will you just please go away?" Rhonda snapped.

Alex studied her face, trying to figure out if the girl suspected anything. Rhonda stared back in furious exasperation, but her fingers were nervously running through her hair and playing with the whistle charm on her necklace. Clearly she was jumpy about running into the guard again. Apparently she'd been so intent on getting out of the store with the stolen earrings that she *hadn't* noticed that the carts were acting like terror on wheels. Or that the doors had turned into the jaws of death. *Lucky for me*, Alex thought with relief.

"Just leave me alone!" Rhonda tried to slip past her.

Alex sidestepped to block her again. "Not until you put those earrings back or pay for them."

"What are you—a frustrated hall monitor? Why don't you go tell your mommy?" Rhonda retorted, looking over Alex's shoulder.

Before Alex could respond, she heard her mother's voice behind her.

"Alex! Where have you been?"

Taking advantage of the interruption, Rhonda headed toward the exit. Reaching into her pocket, she pulled out the earring card, dropped it on the floor, and kept on walking. Alex picked up the card as Rhonda fled through the automatic doors.

Annie lifted the shopping bags and followed Mrs. Mack as she walked up to Alex.

"What've you got there?" Mrs. Mack took the earring card from Alex's hand and held it up to her ear. "They're really darling, Alex, but you don't have pierced ears."

"But I've been thinking about maybe having it done. I can get my ears pierced for free if we buy earrings here." She knew she was babbling but she had to distract her mother. Hopefully Annie would not say anything until Alex had a chance to explain to her sister, in *private*.

Smiling, Mrs. Mack brushed Alex's hair back over her shoulder. "They're your ears, and if you want holes in them, that's up to you. But we don't have time today."

"Right." As Alex turned, she was surprised to see Rhonda standing in the parking lot, staring at her. The girl turned away when she realized Alex had seen her.

Alex's spirits sank as she watched Rhonda cross the lot. *If there's a popularity blacklist at Danielle Atron Junior High, my name's on it now for sure.*

Suddenly a blue Mustang convertible, with its top down, squealed out of a parking space and roared past Rhonda. Meg and Mike shouted as Rhonda veered to get out of their way.

Rhonda will probably blame me for that, too. Sighing, Alex turned to take the earrings back to the jewelry department. All the while she pretended to ignore Annie. But she knew. She felt her sister's eyes on her even as she turned her back toward her.

Annie was glaring at her in silent fury.

CHAPTER 3

Sitting in the backseat, Alex wondered why Annie was so angry with her. Her older sister hadn't spoken to her since leaving the mall.

Not that she'd actually been quiet for even one millisecond up in the front seat, Alex noticed. "I've already got the old paperbacks arranged in boxes," Annie was saying to her mother, then added, "Alphabetically, according to author."

Annie's enthusiasm for the yard sale was surprising. Like their father, Annie preferred the quiet solitude of research that would eventually lead to world recognition for her scientific achievements. Alex herself would rather fill in all the O's on a cereal box for the rest of her days than be stuck in a lab with a bunch of smelly chemicals. *Wonder why the brainiac wants to play salesclerk to a swarm of suburban bargain hunters?* Alex mused. *Oh, I've got it....*

Like Alex, Annie would share in the profits for contributing goods and services.

Plus, Annie was anxious to get the garage cleaned out. She needed more space for her experiments, especially since Alex had become the science project of a lifetime.

"Maybe we can talk Alex into unloading some of her hats," Annie suggested to their mom, as if Alex weren't even sitting in the backseat, two feet away from her. "*Before* the closet shelf collapses."

"That would be entirely up to Alex," Mrs. Mack replied.

As much as she hated to admit it, her sister's idea wasn't such a bad one. Getting rid of a few hats just might make sense, but cleaning the closet was the farthest thing from Alex's mind. Rather, it might be an easy way to raise some quick cash. Some of the hats she'd worn only once, and she could use the money to buy earrings and get her ears pierced.

"Alex?" Mrs. Mack cast a quick glance in the rearview mirror.

"Uh-huh?" Alex answered absently.

"Ray's dad is going to lend us a couple of card tables. Will you go get them sometime tonight?"

"Sure thing, Mom." Anything to stimulate the Mack family economy.

"Everything's down in the garage now," Mrs. Mack continued. "The only thing left is to make and hang the signs, then sort and price the junk."

"Don't call it junk, Mom," Annie corrected. " 'Recycled collectibles' would be more accurate."

When the car pulled into the driveway, Mr. Mack rushed outside. "Where have all of you been? I've been worried!"

"I told you I was taking the girls shopping for yard-sale supplies after school, George." Mrs. Mack kissed her husband affectionately and handed him a shopping bag.

"You did?" Mr. Mack shrugged, then frowned. "What yard sale?"

"The one we're having tomorrow, Dad." Annie gave him the second bag.

"We're having a yard sale? Here?"

"Yes, George," Mrs. Mack said calmly as she steered him toward the house. "Tomorrow."

"That sounds like fun. Why didn't you tell me?"

"I did, sweetheart." Mrs. Mack smiled patiently. George Mack was a dedicated and interested husband and father, but he had a habit of forgetting some of life's little details.

Annie turned toward the garage. "I'll get the tools for the signs, Mom."

"Excellent. Alex can help."

Annie grunted and stalked away. Alex followed, still puzzled by Annie's angry silence. She rounded the corner of the garage just as Annie reached into a pot of red begonias for the key.

"That's just great." Annie straightened and tried the doorknob.

"What's the problem?" Alex asked.

"The key's not in the pot." Annie started for the house.

"No big deal," Alex said. She didn't need a key to get into the garage. A warm tingling swept through her body as she changed from flesh and bone into a puddle of thick, clear jelly.

"Alex, you idiot!" Annie exclaimed.

Flattening her liquid self, Alex flowed under the door and into the garage. After morphing back into herself, she unlocked the door and flung it open to see her sister standing there with a scowl on her face.

"There," Alex said triumphantly. "You're in the garage now, Annie."

"And you'll be in Danielle Atron's lab at Paradise Valley Chemicals before you turn fourteen!" Annie stormed inside. "It would serve you right!"

"What's that supposed to mean?"

"Hey, Alex!" Raymond dragged a card table across the backyard, then turned it sideways to fit it through the door. "Comin' through. Look out."

Annie slammed the door closed behind him. Boxes of stuff for tomorrow's sale blocked the only window, above the sink, and the garage became almost totally dark once the door was closed. Muttering, Annie fumbled for the switch. Alex turned on the lights with a quick zap from her fingers.

"Can't you do *anything* the ordinary way?" Annie's brown eyes flashed.

"She doesn't have to do things the regular way, Annie." Raymond leaned the card table against the washer, then handed Annie the missing key. "So why should she?"

"Because she's getting careless, that's why!" Annie insisted.

"I am not," Alex said.

"Really? You attack people with shopping carts in a store that has surveillance cameras everywhere, and that's not getting careless? You liquefy in the backyard in broad daylight where anyone passing by could see you, and that's not getting careless?"

"No one knows I made the shopping carts move, and no one saw me morph just now," Alex insisted stubbornly. She hadn't thought about surveillance cameras, but she was sure no one could connect her with the rolling carts.

"I saw you morph," Raymond said.

"You don't count," Alex reminded him. "You already know."

"Why did you attack people with shopping carts?" Raymond persisted. "Did one of those twenty-four-hour sales just begin?"

"Yes, why did you?" Annie said. She and Raymond stared at Alex, waiting for an explanation.

"I had to stop Rhonda Clark from leaving the store," Alex said defensively, then wished she'd kept her mouth shut.

"Rhonda Clark?" Raymond cocked his head with interest. "Now, she's a major babe."

Annie sighed. "What was so important, Alex?"

"She was going to shoplift a pair of earrings. So I tried to stop her."

"Why would Rhonda Clark try anything so dumb?" Raymond asked.

"I don't know, Ray."

"That's beside the point anyway," Annie said as she crossed to the tools hanging on the far wall.

"What is the point?" Raymond asked.

"Alex relies on her powers too much."

"I do not!"

"You do, too!" Annie looked back. "Why didn't you just unlock the door with telekinesis, for instance. Why did you have to morph?"

Alex hesitated. She *could* have slid open the bolt with a thought. It just hadn't occurred to her because she was thinking about getting *into* the garage, not *unlocking* the door. So she had transformed into a liquid. Now that she stopped to think about it, morphing was a pretty dumb thing to do.

"Or why use telekinesis at all? Why not go get the spare key from the kitchen? That's what anyone else would have to do."

"Yeah," Raymond said, frowning thoughtfully. "Or you could have broken the window like I did at my house last week."

"Or something," Annie said, throwing up her hands.

"Is that why you're so mad at me, Annie? Because I can do things you can't?"

"Give me a break! I'm *upset* because you're using your powers in public. Sooner or later someone is going to realize that you can do some really weird stuff."

"Like beyond belief," Raymond said.

"And if that happens, it won't be long before Danielle Atron's security goon Vince finds out you're the kid who was contaminated with GC 161." Annie reached for a hammer hanging just beyond her grasp. She pulled over an old piano stool and stepped up onto the wobbly seat.

"I'll get it." Alex began to levitate the hammer.

"No, Alex!"

"But—"

Mounted on small wheels, the piano stool rocked under Annie's weight. Annie put her hand on the wall to steady herself and grabbed the hammer. When she jumped down, the stool shot out from under her and rolled across the floor.

Alex stopped it with her mind before it slammed into her shins.

"See!" Annie shook the hammer at Alex. "You

didn't even try to get out of the way or stop the stool with your hands. You just *thought* it to a stop. So don't tell me you aren't relying on your powers too much!"

Alex looked at the stool and frowned. Her telekinetic response *had* been automatic.

"You're going to turn into some kind of android if you keep this up," Annie said.

"She's right, Alex," Raymond said gravely.

"Who's side are you on, Raymond?" Alex asked.

"Yours," Raymond answered honestly. "I don't want you to become Danielle Atron's prized lab rat, Alex. Using your powers is dangerous."

"It's not just that," Annie said. "Other people have to solve their problems by using their brains." She tapped her head for emphasis. "They don't have your hocus-pocus powers to fall back on. The brain is a muscle that has to be flexed to stay healthy. And your brain, Alex, is turning into a couch potato."

"Would that be baked, fried, or mashed?" Raymond added. "I'm confused."

"Alex, you're forgetting how to think!" Annie exclaimed.

"I am not!" Alex insisted stubbornly.

"You couldn't get through one day without using your powers for something," Annie stated calmly.

"Could, too!"

"Then prove it." Annie jammed the hammer into her belt and planted her hands on her hips. "I dare you to go twenty-four hours without using your powers—for anything."

"Fine," Alex said without hesitation. "You're on."

Annie grinned. "When?"

"Right now is as good a time as any," Alex said.

Annie glanced at her watch. "I've got five-fourteen."

Raymond adjusted the time on his own watch. "Five-fourteen."

The old clock over the dryer also said five-fourteen.

"Counting down to five-fifteen," Raymond said. "Thirty seconds."

How hard could it be? Alex figured, then noticed her sister's smug smile. Annie didn't think she could do it, and neither did Raymond, but Alex knew better. She had been plain, old, ordinary Alexandra Mack a lot longer than she had been Alex Mack the wonder girl.

Not using my powers should be easy, Alex assured herself.

The hammer began to slide out from under

Annie's belt as the older girl shifted her weight. Alex saw it and opened her mouth in warning.

"Five, four . . ." Raymond counted aloud.

"Annie, the hammer—" Alex pointed.

Annie frowned back at her, not listening.

"Three, two, one!" Raymond looked up. "Project Potato Head begins!"

Starting now, Alex thought as she watched the heavy tool slip out of Annie's belt and fall on her foot.

"Ow!" Wincing, Annie grabbed her injured foot.

Alex met Annie's annoyed gaze. "Twenty-four hours. No powers. Not for anything."

Annie stuck her hand out and the two sisters shook.

Piece of cake, Alex thought with a triumphant grin.

CHAPTER 4

"Scott did that?" Alex laughed aloud and almost fell off the kitchen chair. She was talking to her friend Robyn on the phone, her feet propped up on the table. "Why?"

"Someone dared him, and you know Scott," Robyn said.

Not well enough, Alex thought with a wistful sigh. Scott was this unbelievably cute eighth-grade guy she'd had her eye on all year.

"You really should have been there, Alex."

"I wish!" Alex would have loved seeing Scott doing backflips down the aisle of a movie theater that afternoon. Instead she watched runaway shopping carts roll down the aisle of a department store. But she couldn't share this once-in-a-lifetime experience with Robyn—her friend knew nothing about her powers, and it had to stay that way. But Alex told Robyn just about everything else that ever happened to her.

"What about doing the mall tomorrow?" Robyn asked. "Burns is having a sale on the top ten CDs."

"Can't," Alex grumbled. "The yard sale's tomorrow, and my mom says I have to help. One of those family activities, you know?"

"Oh, yeah. I forgot." Robyn sighed. "Too bad."

"Alex!" Mrs. Mack yelled from the living room. "Your signs aren't done, and it'll be dark soon!"

"In a minute, Mom!" Alex yelled back.

"Now!"

"Sorry, Robyn. Gotta go."

"Yeah, well, maybe Nicole and I can hang with you awhile in the morning. Catch ya later, Alex."

"Right. Later." Rising slowly, Alex hung up the phone. She didn't want to make signs tonight or sell junk tomorrow. She wanted to spend the time with her friends.

"Come on, honey," Mrs. Mack urged from the

doorway. "This'll be fun. You'll see." She smiled and turned away.

Not hardly, Alex thought as she trudged out of the kitchen. *Shopping for CDs at the mall—now that would be fun. Who wanted to watch other people shop—for stuff we trashed a long time ago?* Alex went into the living room to finish her signs. Her mother stood in the middle of the room, holding a sweater out in front of her as if she didn't want to get too close to it.

"But I've had that sweater since high school, Barbara," Mr. Mack pleaded as she picked lint off the gray pullover. "It's my favorite."

Alex couldn't help giggling as she sat on the floor by the cardboard and markers. Every once in a while her mother threatened to throw out their father's old, ragged sweater with holes in the elbows. Mr. Mack always talked her out of it.

"All right, George." Mrs. Mack sighed and handed her husband his precious sweater. "But the warped tennis racket and the moldy combat boots have got to go."

"And don't forget that old stuffed rooster in the garage," Annie reminded her mother with a wink at Alex.

"That, too." Mrs. Mack crossed her arms and fixed Mr. Mack with a no-nonsense stare.

"But I won that at the Martin County Fair when I was ten!" Mr. Mack looked at his wife aghast.

"We know, Dad," Alex said gently. "But it's so ancient you can't even tell it's a rooster anymore. Looks more like a plucked chicken."

"Ever since you washed it two years ago, it's smelled so bad we couldn't standing having it in the house," Annie added.

"No discussion this time, George."

"Okay." Mr. Mack shuffled into the kitchen, muttering to himself. "It's the only thing I've ever won."

"You're not really gonna try to sell that stuff, are you, Mom?" Alex drew a big exclamation point on the sign with her black marker and added the dot with a flourish.

"Of course not. I'll probably have to throw them out when he's not looking, but your father will feel better about losing those things if he thinks someone paid money for them."

"There. Finished." Alex held up the sign.

"Good. The letters are big so you can read it from a distance," Mrs. Mack said with an approving smile. "How many do we have?"

"Twelve counting this one." Annie outlined a black arrow in red, then capped the marker. "That should be enough."

"That's all you'll have time to put up anyway." Mrs. Mack took the last two signs and stapled them to pointed stakes. "It'll be dark in less than an hour."

Annie handed Alex six of the signs and a hammer. "Plenty of time if we split the neighborhood in half," Annie said.

Once outside Annie paused before heading toward the corner on the left. "On your honor, Alex. No powers. I'll come help you after I finish, okay?"

"I can pound a few stakes into the ground without my powers or your help, Annie."

"Just checking."

"Not necessary," Alex said indignantly. "I said I wouldn't use them, and I won't. Period." Turning, she jogged to the corner and positioned a sign in the ground, its arrow pointing toward the house.

The first two signs went into the ground easily. However, the dirt was as hard as cement on the third corner. Alex pounded until the stake broke. Finally she leaned the sign against a big rock and braced it in front with several smaller stones. The sun had dipped below the horizon by the time she finished placing the fourth and fifth signs.

In the darkening twilight, Alex looked up the street toward the last and final corner. No one was out walking a dog. No kids played in front yards. No elderly couples sat on front porches. No cars went by and no lawn mowers roared. *The street sure is deserted*, Alex thought. *Maybe, just to be on the safe side, I should use my powers to put this last sign up.* That way she wouldn't even have to walk up the empty street. Alex sighed. *Officer Annie could appear at any moment and serve me a citation for using my powers.*

Anxious to be finished and on her way home, Alex jogged up the street and pushed the last sign into the soft ground. As she raised the hammer to drive the stake deeper, a twig snapped behind her. She whirled to face the high, thick hedge that formed a barrier between the sidewalk and a two-story house.

"Who's there?" Alex's voice shook slightly and seemed to echo in the silence. No one answered. She listened, but there was no noise—anywhere. Not even crickets chirped to break the creepy quiet.

Her mother's constant warnings about being out alone after dark flashed through her mind.

The streetlight above her buzzed and flashed on.

Startled, Alex gasped aloud and jumped. Heart pounding against her ribs, she clutched the hammer like a club, but nothing weird leaped out of the shadows to grab her. Convinced that she was spooking herself with an overactive imagination, Alex hit the stake until it was secure, then hurried back across the street toward home.

The streetlights were widely spaced and offered little pockets of lighted safety separated by long stretches of ominous dark. Halfway down the next block Alex thought she heard footsteps behind her. She glanced back. No one was there. At least, not that she could see. Dark shadows and clumps of bushes on landscaped lawns provided perfect hiding places for someone watching her.

Alex thought she heard a rustling sound in the juniper shrubs on her right and quickened her step.

Was someone watching her? She had always thought her mother was being overly cautious with her warnings. Paradise Valley was a peaceful town with a crime rate of almost zero. Now, though, Alex didn't feel so safe. She *felt* as if she was being watched. The very idea made her really nervous . . . and being really nervous made her glow, another side effect of the experimental GC 161 compound.

Her skin started to shine with a golden light as Alex ran toward the next corner. She didn't dare try to hide in the bushes or shadows. Someone— or some *thing*—might be lurking there, waiting to deal her a fate worse than anything Danielle Atron could think up. She *might* be able to explain why she was glowing if anyone saw her—say she was a member of a Thomas Edison cult or something. But what could she do if someone really dangerous came along?

She could zap them or send them flying through the air or turn herself into a puddle of Jell-O and escape, that's what she could do.

Forget Annie's dare. If she was in real danger, Alex could use her powers. She could plead self-defense to Annie. Her sister would understand, wouldn't she?

Why hang around long enough to find out? Alex decided. She bolted around the corner and collided with a solid body. A shriek of fright rose in her throat as she stumbled backward and almost fell. The other person faltered, then walked out of the dark shadows into the light.

"*Annie!*" Alex cried out.

A scowl furrowed Annie's face. "Alex, you're glowing!"

"I know, Annie! Someone's following me!"

"Seriously?" Annie peered around the corner. Her frown deepened when she looked back at Alex. "I don't see anyone, *but* you certainly could attract a crowd lit up like the Statue of Liberty."

"You know I start to glow whenever I'm really nervous." Alex looked at her hands and tried to calm herself. The glow began to fade slowly. "And glowing doesn't count as a power, either. I can't help it."

"Okay, I'll give you that. Glowing doesn't count, but try to relax, okay? What if someone sees you?" Annie quickly guided Alex off the sidewalk and behind a large tree.

"I heard someone, Annie. Really."

"Well, there's no one there now. It was probably just your imagination."

"Maybe. Maybe not." Still spooked, Alex shivered.

"No one's following you, Alex. Now calm down so you stop shining like a Christmas tree and we can go home."

"Someone's out there!" Alex insisted.

"I don't think so." Annie pulled Alex back onto the sidewalk and looked at her intensely. "You really want to prove that I'm wrong about relying on your powers too much, right?"

"Yeah ... so?"

"Well, I think you're just overreacting to not using them."

"Huh?" Alex blinked, confused.

"Scientists have studied conditioning in controlled experiments with monkeys. When the monkeys were separated from a familiar object, they exhibited atypical behaviors such as—"

"What does that have to do with me?" Alex asked, exasperated. "Do you see me swinging from trees?"

"You're imagining things, Alex. It's because you're feeling vulnerable without your powers." Annie cocked her head. "You're skin is just about back to normal. Let's go before Mom starts to worry."

Alex hesitated as Annie turned and headed down the sidewalk. As much as she hated to admit it, Annie might be right. Maybe she was letting her imagination get the best of her.

But maybe, just for once, Annie was wrong.

CHAPTER 5

Alex and Annie walked in the front door and found
the living room a disaster area. Mrs. Mack was ar-
ranging household items into piles according to
price, and there was barely enough room to weave
through the mounds of junk and heaps of clothes.
Alex picked her way carefully around three roller
skates of various sizes. Their mates had all vanished
long ago, never to be seen again.

"What do you think, George?" Mrs. Mack held
up a pink bud vase that had been sitting in the
back of a kitchen cupboard for as long as Alex
could remember. "A dollar?"

Mr. Mack lowered the evening paper, glanced at the vase, and said, "Fifty cents."

"Where'd that come from anyway?" Alex asked.

"It was a valentine gift from an old college boy-friend." Mrs. Mack winked and glanced at Mr. Mack. "Someone I knew before your father swept me off my feet."

"Rodney Brooks," Mr. Mack said without looking up.

"George!" Mrs. Mack exclaimed. "You remember Rodney?"

"My main competition for your charming attention? Of course I remember." Lowering the paper, Mr. Mack eyed the pink vase again. "Twenty-five cents is more like it."

Mrs. Mack cocked her head, studying the vase. "Twenty-five cents it is. I should have thrown it out years ago anyway."

Mr. Mack pulled a quarter out of his pocket. "Sold."

Puzzled, Mrs. Mack took the quarter and handed her husband the vase. He grinned, blew her a kiss, and promptly dropped the vase in the wastebasket by his chair.

Mrs. Mack blinked, then smiled.

Annie raised an eyebrow.

Looking extremely pleased with himself, Mr. Mack shook his paper and started reading again.

Alex giggled. *So much for Mom's old boyfriend, Rodney Brooks,* she thought.

"So what do you want us to do now?" Annie asked.

Mrs. Mack picked up a list from the coffee table. "Well, we still need to get the card tables from Raymond's father."

"Ray already brought them over," Alex said. "They're in the garage."

Mrs. Mack checked card tables off her list. "Okay. Let's see. Wash the old glasses and dishes. Alex can do that, and Annie can help me sort and price the clothes."

"Aye, aye, sir!" Alex snapped to attention, then pivoted and marched toward the kitchen.

Mismatched plates, cups, and glasses were stacked on the counter. Alex opened the dishwasher and began putting them inside. As she picked up the last glass, she heard a noise outside the back door and looked up.

Dark eyes in a white face stared at her through the window.

Alex gasped and dropped the glass. She instantly reached out with her mind to save it, then stopped herself. *No powers for twenty-four hours, Alex.* The glass shattered on the floor, and she jumped away from it. When Alex glanced back at the window, the face was gone.

"Are you okay, Alex?" Mr. Mack ran into the kitchen and skidded to a halt. The floor was covered with broken glass.

"Yes, but—"

"Did you cut yourself?" Mrs. Mack asked as she skirted the glass to reach the broom and dustpan stored beside the refrigerator.

"No, but—"

"Only one casualty?" Annie paused in the doorway and leaned against the frame. "One out of ten. Not bad, Alex."

Ignoring Annie, Alex grabbed her father's hand. "Someone's out there, Dad!"

"Who? Where?" Mr. Mack's eyes narrowed.

"There!" Alex pointed toward the window. "Someone was watching me."

Mrs. Mack frowned. "Just now?"

"Relax, Dad," Annie said with a bored sigh. "No one's watching her, and no one was following her earlier, either."

"What?" Mrs. Mack dropped the dustpan. Splinters of glass bounced out of it and back onto the floor.

"Maybe someone was following me," Alex said sheepishly. "I'm not sure. I heard noises and thought someone was sneaking up on me, but . . . maybe not."

Annie turned to their stricken mother. "Really, Mom. I was there, and I didn't hear or see anyone. Alex's imagination is just working overtime tonight, like her brain's on overload or something."

"But I'm positive I just saw someone looking at me through the window," Alex insisted. "I swear."

"Well, I think I'll go check. Just to be sure," Mr. Mack said, grabbing a flashlight from the closet.

"Thanks, Dad." Alex went to the window to watch as her father searched the yard and around the house with the flashlight. She was sure she had seen a face at the window.

But who?

"Why don't you come into the living room with us, Alex?" Mrs. Mack suggested, squeezing Alex's shoulder.

Annie turned to survey the chaos in the living room. "You can help us with inventory," she said to her sister.

"Come on, Alex," Mrs. Mack coaxed.

"In a minute, Mom." Alex smiled to calm her mother's fears, then shuffled to the counter and reached for the box of detergent under the sink. "I still have to run the dishwasher."

"Don't be long. I want you to write out the price tags."

"Sure." Alex poured detergent into the plastic cups on the dishwasher door. Her father came back inside a moment after her mother left. Alex looked at him expectantly.

"I can't find anyone, Alex." Mr. Mack set the flashlight on the kitchen table. "If someone was out there, he's long gone now. Nothing to worry about, okay?"

"If?" Alex stared at him. "I'm not seeing things, Dad! You've got to believe me."

"Now, I didn't say you were seeing things," Mr. Mack said patiently. "But maybe it wasn't a *someone*. Maybe it was a *something*. The reflection of a headlight or a piece of paper. Your eyes playing tricks on you. It happens to everyone."

He doesn't believe me, either! If Annie the scientist said she saw something, everyone would believe it was a fact. Alex opened her mouth to argue, then thought better of it. No one would believe her unless she had proof.

Considering the problem settled, Mr. Mack patted her arm and headed for the living room. "Coming, Alex?"

"In a second." Alone again, Alex wrapped her arms around herself and began to pace. Although she couldn't be certain that someone had been following her when she was putting out the yard-sale signs, she was positively, absolutely sure she had seen someone at the window. It hadn't been a reflection or a loose piece of paper. She had seen a face.

But whose face?

Hidden in the dark outside, the face had also been distorted by the kitchen light reflecting off the window glass. She couldn't identify the peeping Tom, and she couldn't even begin to guess who would want to frighten her. Why would someone be out to get her? The chemical company hadn't been snooping around in a while. What had she done to anyone lately . . . ?

Rhonda?

Alex felt a surge of relief. Although Rhonda had acted as if she wanted to get caught at the mall, maybe she had decided that getting arrested for shoplifting was pretty dumb, and now she didn't want anyone to know! Maybe Rhonda was afraid she would tell someone and ruin her reputation!

"Like I'd start the rumor and risk getting known as a snitch," Alex muttered.

Actually, Alex decided, maybe Rhonda just wanted to talk to her, to make *sure* she wouldn't tell anyone. Maybe that's why she followed her. And maybe it was kind of hard for her to admit that she was going to shoplift. It wasn't the kind of thing that was easy to talk about.

The quickest way to find out, Alex figured, was to call Rhonda up and give her a chance to explain. *And then I can tell her that I won't blab about what happened to anyone. After all, I know all about keeping secrets. That way Rhonda won't tell the whole world I'm a dorky tattletale.*

Anxious to assure Rhonda that her secret was safe, Alex rushed to the wall phone. They might still end up as friends. Or, at the very least, she could save her suffering social status from an early death.

Sifting through the stack of phone books piled on the counter, Alex grabbed the junior high directory and flipped it open. She found Rhonda Clark's number and dialed.

As the phone rang, Alex slapped her forehead.

Duh, Alex! Rhonda lived on the other side of town. She hadn't had time to get home yet. Alex started to hang up, but someone answered on the second ring.

"Hello?"

It sounded just like Rhonda!

Alex's heart jumped, and she whispered, "Rhonda?"

"Yeah. Who's this?" Rhonda asked suspiciously.

Alex slammed the phone down. If Rhonda was home, that meant . . . no.

Alex started shaking. It could mean only one thing.

Someone else had been at the window!

Who? Really scared now, Alex paced and wondered. Maybe someone suspected she had unusual powers and was trying to catch her in the act. Maybe that someone was Vince of Paradise Chemical Plant Security. He was in charge of trying to find the kid who had taken a GC 161 shower. Maybe he *knew* it was her, but he didn't have solid evidence!

Alex glanced fearfully at the window and shuddered. Suddenly the peaceful, quiet neighborhood seemed treacherous and filled with unknown terrors. If she had used her powers to stop the glass from falling, Vince would have seen! *A close call*, she thought with a shiver of dread.

After turning on the dishwasher, Alex headed for the living room. Annie didn't know it, but she had done Alex a huge favor by daring her not to use her powers for a day. Now Alex had an even better reason for not using them.

Someone was watching her.

CHAPTER 6

When Alex awoke the next morning, she felt pretty silly about being so scared the night before. Warm sunlight streamed through her bedroom window, and the bright blue sky was dotted with a few powder-puff clouds. Nothing lurked in the morning shadows around the house, and no evil eyes peered at her from behind bushes.

Alex dressed and went downstairs. The aroma of brewing coffee filled the kitchen and Alex with a sense of well-being. Everyone was cheerful and excited about the yard sale.

"An even split?" Annie was saying to her father. "Four ways?"

"That seems only fair," Mr. Mack said, taking a sip of hot coffee. "This is a family project, and the profits should be divided evenly." He glanced at Mrs. Mack. "What do you think?"

Mrs. Mack was unloading the old glasses and plates from the dishwasher. "I think we'd better get moving or there won't be any profits to split."

"I won't argue with that." Annie stood up and pushed a metal box toward her father. "We can use this as a cashbox."

"Don't you keep your secret theories and science-project notes locked up in this, Annie?" Mr. Mack asked.

Annie handed him the keys and grinned. "I think those papers will be safe from scientific espionage for a day, Dad."

"No one else can understand them anyway," Alex added.

"Very true." Mr. Mack took the cashbox outside.

Annie followed, then paused before closing the back door. "Whoa! The Weather Channel said it was going to be hot today, but it must be eighty already."

"Think the heat will keep people away?" Alex asked.

"Don't think so," Annie said. "Two cars just pulled up."

"But it's not time yet!"

"Bargain hunters don't care, Alex. Here." Mrs. Mack held out a cardboard box filled with clean dishes. "Find a place for these on one of the tables, okay?"

"Will do, Mom." As Alex helped haul boxes out of the living room to the yard, her fears from the night before disappeared almost completely. In fact, the more she thought about it, the more she began to suspect that Annie was right—again. Her imagination had run wild, turning perfectly harmless noises and shadows into a threat that didn't exist.

Mrs. Mack peered into the third box Alex lugged out and frowned. Holding an old dusty frame up to the light, she said, "Would you go get the glass cleaner, Alex? And some paper towels."

"And two folding chairs from the garage," her father added.

"Right away." Alex ran to the kitchen to get the cleaner first. The phone rang as she pulled the plastic bottle out from under the sink.

"Hello." Alex tucked the phone between her chin and shoulder to reach for a roll of paper towels.

A shrill, high-pitched sound screeched from the receiver.

Alex jumped back and the phone fell from her shoulder onto the counter. Ears ringing, Alex stared at the receiver as the screech continued. It ended abruptly when the line clicked and went dead.

With a shaky hand Alex hung up the phone and stood still for a moment, deep in thought. The shrill noise seemed vaguely familiar, like a scream or maybe a whistle.

A faulty connection or a deliberate prank? Alex wondered uneasily. She waited a couple of minutes to see if anyone called back. The phone remained ominously silent, but a loud thud sounded in the garage.

Alex inhaled sharply and snapped her head around. The door leading from the kitchen into the garage was closed. Tucking the glass cleaner and paper towels under one arm, Alex cautiously approached the door and placed her ear against it. All was quiet for several seconds. Then she thought she heard footsteps.

Someone was in the garage!

Alex went rigid, then rolled her eyes, laughing at her own foolishness. The someone was probably Annie or her father. Maybe they had gotten tired of waiting for the lawn chairs. And, she decided, the strange phone call had probably been nothing but a weird malfunction in the lines.

Alex opened the door, expecting to see the lawn chairs missing from their hooks high on the far wall. The chairs were still there, and the side door to the outside was open.

Doesn't mean anything, Alex told herself as she hurried to the open door and looked out. No one was in sight, but a creepy feeling bristled the hairs on her neck.

Her hands were still shaky as she set down the cleaner and towels. She glanced at the folding metal chairs. Flustered and preoccupied, she began to reach for them with her mind. As they started to rise into the air, she quickly shut off her thoughts. The chairs fell back on the hooks and wobbled above her.

Furious with herself, Alex took a deep breath. "What am I doing?" she said out loud. "Snap out of it, Alexandra!"

Maybe Annie was right about her dependence

on her powers. It had happened so automatically. Fortunately, Annie wasn't there to notice.

Alex dragged the stepladder beside the sink and opened it. Her troubled thoughts nagged her as she climbed toward the chairs.

She *had* gotten use to being able to move things with her mind and zap electric lights and appliances on and off from a distance. It sure did come in handy when she had to clean her side of the room! And although she didn't turn herself into a blob of clear jelly very often, being able to liquefy had gotten her out of some sticky situations now and then. Sometimes she morphed in the bathtub just because it was fun. Luckily the gelatin didn't dissolve in water, and being adrift in the tub was a nice way to zone out for a while.

There was no escaping the truth. Using her powers had become as natural to her as breathing.

A new determination filled Alex as she braced her hips against the top step of the ladder and grabbed the nearest chair. Yes, she wanted to show Annie she could get along just fine without morphing, zapping, or using telekinesis. But suddenly it was something she had to prove to herself, too. If she couldn't get through one lousy day without using her powers, she'd never have confidence in herself again.

As Alex lifted the chair off the hook, she realized that the nylon mesh and metal tubing construction was heavier than she had thought. She couldn't hold it. The chair fell against the large sink below, pulling Alex down with it. She stumbled down the ladder steps and barely saved herself from falling on the concrete floor by grabbing the rim of the metal sink.

The piles of boxes that had been stacked in the sink yesterday were gone. As she righted herself, Alex glanced out the window.

A figure dressed in dark clothes ducked behind a storage shed in the neighbors' yard.

Alex frowned. Her eyes were not playing tricks on her *this* time! Someone *was* spying on her! And no one could convince her otherwise.

"What is taking you so long, Alex?" Annie burst into the garage through the kitchen door.

"Someone's hiding behind the Hendersons' shed, Annie! Watching me!"

Shaking her head, Annie picked up the fallen chair off the floor and leaned it against the sink. "Don't you ever quit?"

"I'm not kidding, Annie! I saw someone!"

"Really?" Annie's brows knit together.

"Yes, really." Alex pointed to the window. "Look for yourself."

Easing around the sink, Annie looked out the window from an angle so she wouldn't be seen. Her worried brow vanished, and she relaxed with a slight shake of her head. "He's a real threat, all right."

"Who?" Alex peered out the window and winced. Eight-year-old Ronnie Henderson was in his backyard, wearing a dark baseball uniform and swinging a bat. Mr. Henderson came out and waved the boy toward the car.

"Remember what happened to the boy who cried wolf, Alex."

"Ronnie's not who I—" Alex decided to shut up. She knew the small boy wasn't the dark figure she had seen by the shed, but she couldn't prove it. Arguing with Annie would be a waste of time and effort.

"What happened to this?" Annie pointed to the chair by the sink. One arm was bent at an odd angle.

"I dropped it," Alex answered honestly. "I didn't know it was so heavy—and I couldn't use my powers to stop it from falling," she added defiantly.

Annie motioned toward the chair still hanging on the wall. "Let's get the other one down. We've already got customers, and Dad wants to sit down to take their money."

Moving the ladder under the second chair, Alex scrambled upward. Grabbing the metal frame with both hands, she carefully lowered the chair down to her sister.

"Now, that wasn't so hard, was it?" Taking both chairs, Annie left without waiting for a reply.

Sometimes Annie's sarcasm annoyed Alex. But right now she was more upset that Annie didn't believe her when she said someone was spying on her.

Collecting the glass cleaner and paper towels, Alex left through the outside door and closed it behind her. She paused to stare at the Hendersons' storage shed. She *had* seen someone else. She was sure of it.

Impulsively Alex took off running across the lawn. If someone was spying on her from the Hendersons' yard, she had to know. As she ran, Alex realized she'd be totally defenseless if that someone was still hanging around. Then she remembered the bottle of glass cleaner she was carrying.

Not totally defenseless. . . .

Alex's fingers closed around the plastic spray lever. She dashed toward the storage shed, holding the bottle in front of her. If nothing else, squirting the unsuspecting watcher would buy her time to run away.

Flattening herself against the shed, she inched her way to the corner. When she got to the end of the wall, she gripped her spray bottle and took a deep breath.

"Gotcha!" Alex shouted as she leaped around the corner of the small building . . . and showered a fine mist of glass cleaner over a wheelbarrow, a rake, and a shovel.

No black-clad anybody crouched behind the shed.

Alex froze, disappointed at first and then relieved. Either she had imagined the mysterious person or that person was just the Henderson kid. Her shoulders slumped as she realized the truth.

Annie was right again.

After all, Annie was right so often, why wouldn't she be right this time, too?

Being powerless was making her nervous. It

was like being a new Alex all over again. Or more like being the old Alex. The Alex that was just an ordinary kid, with no special talents, just a regular sort of girl. And now she'd have to learn to rely on that kid. She'd have to learn to trust herself. No one was really following her. She was just scared about being on her own. Next time she thought she saw or heard someone, she'd keep her mouth shut.

As she ran toward the front yard, Alex had to laugh at herself. She had sure shown those garden tools who was top spray bottle in this neighborhood.

CHAPTER 7

"You're actually going to sell these gorgeous clogs?" Nicole asked Alex. Nicole held up the red clogs and looked at her friend as if she had lost her mind.

"They're too small for me," Alex explained. "I walk right out of them when I wear them. Four dollars and they're yours."

Shaking her head, Nicole put them back on the table next to an old piggy bank that was missing an ear. "You sure do drive a hard bargain, Alex. Four bucks for old, worn-out, scuffed-up—"

"But you just said they were gorgeous," Robyn pointed out.

"I'll give them to you for three," Alex offered.
Nicole made a face.

Robyn shaded her eyes from the sun. "I didn't know it was going to be so hot today," she said. "And I forgot to put sunscreen on. I'll be a lobster in no time." Robyn was a pale-skinned redhead.

Alex found a tube of sunscreen that her mother had brought out and gave it to Robyn. "And here, take these," Nicole said, placing her white-framed sunglasses on Robyn's nose.

"Thanks, that's better," Robyn said as she slathered sunscreen on her arms.

"It *is* awfully hot out," Alex said. "Especially for this early in the morning. I wish there was some shade here on the front lawn." She eyed the baseball cap that Nicole was wearing and thought about going in to get one of her own.

Nicole slipped the clogs on and was testing them by walking up and down the driveway. Avoiding the other shoppers who had come early to bargain hunt, she clomped up the walkway and said to Alex and Robyn, "What do you think? Are they me?"

"Definitely," Robyn said.

"I was going to buy a CD at the mall today," Nicole said. "If I buy these clogs, too, I'll be no better than all the other consumer queens out there who live to shop."

Robyn and Alex exchanged glances and rolled their eyes. They'd heard it all before.

Checking out Nicole's cap, an idea formed in Alex's head. That hat was purple corduroy—she didn't own one like it. "Hey, Nicole, don't you think that baseball cap would be a nice addition to my collection?" Alex asked her friend, who was still trying out the red clogs. "It looks like it would fit me perfectly."

"I'd say about as perfect as these clogs fit me," Nicole said, a sparkle in her eye.

Alex laughed. "It's a deal." She held her hand out, and Nicole slapped her five. Then she took her purple cap off and placed it on Alex's head.

"Ah, shade. Just what I needed," Alex said, pulling the brim down.

"Speaking of shade," Robyn said, "I don't think I'm going to be able to part with these sunglasses, Nicole. What if I trade you this bracelet for the glasses?"

"Deal!" Nicole said, taking the friendship bracelet from Robyn.

"I'm really glad you guys came over today to keep me company," Alex said.

"No *problema*," Nicole said. "Even though I despise suburban commercialism, at least we traded merchandise instead of contributing to the already-bloated capitalist system."

"Don't tell my sister that," Alex whispered. "She thinks we should be sharing all the booty here. She wants the money to buy something exciting like a lifetime supply of petri dishes."

"Okay, Al," Nicole said. "We won't breathe a word."

"We'd better get going to the mall now anyway. My mother is going to meet us there in a while and give us a ride home," Robyn said. "Thanks for the sunscreen."

"Thanks for the clogs," Nicole added.

"Thanks for the baseball cap."

"Thanks for the sunglasses."

Laughing, the girls all said goodbye, and Alex was left alone. She hadn't said anything to her friends about being watched and followed. Somehow, trying to explain without mentioning her powers and the chemical plant's determination to identify her made the whole thing seem kind of melodramatic, if not downright wacko. Neither Nicole nor Robyn knew about the GC 161 and the strange side effects. And it had to stay that way, for their safety as well as Alex's. But having them around was great anyway, to take her mind off her problems.

Alex looked over at Annie, who was selling a broken phone to a young guy in his early twenties who looked as if he'd just rolled out of bed. Alex knew for a fact that the phone didn't ring. You could dial out, but you couldn't receive any calls. Alex had to laugh. Annie could sell ice to a penguin. *Maybe the guy's antisocial*, Alex mused, *and only wants to use the phone to order out pizza.*

"Quench your thirst for a quarter!" Raymond's voice rose above the yard sale chatter.

Alex glanced toward the Alvarados' yard, where Raymond had set up a lemonade stand to cash in on the Macks' customer traffic. His business was thriving under the hot sun. When he wasn't pouring and collecting money, he was running back and forth to his house to refill his pitchers. Nicole and Robyn had stopped to buy a drink, and Raymond talked them into staying while he went inside for yet another refill.

Mrs. Mack moved through the impressive crowd of browsers, answering questions and bartering with smiling graciousness. Her public relations training was being put to good use, as was Mr. Mack's number-crunching background.

He sat in the shade of a tree with the cashbox, making change and recording every transaction on his laptop computer.

Annie had just said goodbye to the antisocial pizza eater, after giving him a three-year-old phone book to go with the phone. Alex didn't notice Annie strolling over toward her—her eyes were riveted on the pitcher full of pink lemonade and ice across the lawn, and she was trying not to salivate.

"Don't you know the difference between a swap meet and a yard sale?" Annie said as she came up behind Alex. "This is supposed to be a profit-making enterprise."

Oh, well, one less petri dish for Annie, Alex thought to herself, ignoring her sister. She'd hoped that Annie hadn't seen the exchange between her and her friends.

"I mean I'm glad you and your friends are now properly accessorized, but how are you going to make any money if you give everything away?" Annie persisted.

Maybe I should try to sell some of this junk, Alex said to herself. She hadn't forgotten about the pierced earrings she'd found in the department store. Plus, she wanted to prove to Annie that she could make money for the family, too.

As Annie zeroed in on a man rummaging through a pile of miscellaneous hardware, Alex donned a bright smile and moved toward a young boy of about five standing three feet away. His mother was nowhere to be seen. The boy picked up a hammer and hit the edge of the table. Tools and hardware bounced and rattled.

"Don't do that," Alex said sternly.

The boy hammered even harder, sending a large coffee can full of nuts and bolts bouncing off the table. Alex stooped to pick up the scattered items, and thankfully the boy put down the hammer. But next he reached for the sharp, toothed side of a rusty saw blade.

Alex could have stopped the boy's hand with a thought, but she didn't. Instead, she jumped up and grabbed him by the wrist before he touched the blade and cut himself.

The boy shrieked and howled.

Everyone in the yard turned to look.

A woman wearing a baggy T-shirt and worn jeans charged Alex like a mother bear racing to defend her cub. Red-faced with anger, she stuck her face inches from Alex's. "Just what do you think you're doing?"

Stunned, Alex let go of the boy and stammered. "The saw blade—it's uh, sharp and—"

Too angry to listen, the woman wheeled around and left, dragging the boy by the hand.

Annie sidled up to Alex's side. "She almost bought that old vegetable slicer-dicer thing that never worked right. Oh, well."

"What was that all about, Alex?" Mrs. Mack asked calmly.

"I was afraid he'd cut himself on the saw blade. That's all, Mom. Honest."

Mrs. Mack nodded and smiled. "Don't worry about it, okay?"

"Okay. Thanks." Alex strolled past a painting of a poodle on velvet and looked around for another potential customer. An elderly man and woman were pulling books out of the end box, glancing at the covers, and then tossing them aside.

Alex decided to ask if she could help them find something in particular. However, just as she reached the table, the couple turned to leave and the woman's shoulder bag strap snagged on a torn edge of the cardboard box.

"Look out!" Alex shouted the warning as she grabbed the box to keep it from falling.

Startled, the old woman stumbled backward. Because Alex was holding the box with the trapped purse strap, the shoulder bag was yanked from the woman's grasp.

Alex quickly pulled the strap free.

"My purse!" The woman screamed as she turned and saw Alex holding her bag. She leaped forward to snatch it back, tripped over a roller skate, and collapsed.

The old man grabbed his wife by the arms to stop her fall. Suddenly he stiffened and put a hand to his side. Apparently he'd wrenched his back. Moaning in pain, he let go, and the woman crumpled to the ground with a yelp of surprise.

Alex watched the entire episode in open-mouthed astonishment. Everything happened so fast, she couldn't move quickly enough to help them—not without her powers.

"My goodness! What happened?" Mrs. Mack rushed to the old couple's aid. She glanced anxiously at the old man, who was bent over with his hand on his back.

"That girl tried to steal my purse, then tripped

me!" The woman glared at Alex as Mrs. Mack gently helped her to her feet.

"No, I didn't!" Wide-eyed, Alex pleaded with her mother. "Her purse got caught on the box, and then she tripped on a roller skate!"

"Oh, now it's *my* fault!" the woman snapped indignantly. Jutting out her chin, she limped past her husband. "Come on, Albert. We're leaving."

"Yes, dear."

"I want you to call our lawyer as soon as we get home, Albert. We'll sue. That's what!"

"Yes, dear."

Sighing, Mrs. Mack glanced away from the elderly couple wobbling toward the street and fixed Alex with a questioning stare.

"I didn't do anything, Mom," Alex said defensively. "They were flinging books all over the place, and she didn't notice that her purse strap—"

"Okay, Alex, okay." Mrs. Mack held her hands up. "There's something else you can do for me. Come on."

Alex had the uncomfortable feeling that her mother didn't believe she wasn't to blame, but she followed her silently. They made their way across the lawn to where Mr. Mack was counting change into a man's hand. "Eight, nine, and ten." He smiled wistfully at the stack of old forty-five records the man had purchased. "I'm sure you'll enjoy listening to those records. They're classics. I don't have a phonograph anymore, or I wouldn't be selling them."

"Don't plan on listening to them," the man said as he picked up the stack. "I want them for target practice." He turned abruptly before Alex could react and walked right into her.

Alex froze as the man looked her in the eye.

Vince!

"What are you staring at?" Vince snapped as he backed away from her. The head of security at Paradise Valley Chemical never seemed to be in a good mood.

"N-nothing. I just, uh—sorry."

"Don't stare, Alex," Mrs. Mack whispered after Vince nodded and left. "It's rude."

"Sorry," Alex muttered again. Her mother didn't know she had good reason to be afraid of Vince. Had Annie seen him, too? Alex scanned the yard and saw Annie run through the front door carrying a green sweater she had gotten last Christmas. It looked brand-new because she'd never worn it. She handed the sweater to a woman who gave her cash in return.

Mr. Mack looked accusingly at his wife. "Vince is going to destroy my records!"

"They're his records now, George."

"Annie!" Alex waved her over before she got involved in another sale.

Annie appeared and gave Mr. Mack the sweater money. Then she turned to her sister. "What is it, Alex?"

"Vince was just here." Alex gave Annie a pointed look.

"He was?" Trying not to look alarmed, Annie shrugged. "Vince was here, huh, Dad?"

"Yeah. He saw the yard sale flyer on the cafeteria bulletin board." Mr. Mack sighed despondently. "I didn't know he wanted old records for target practice when he asked me if I had any."

"Forget the records, George." Mrs. Mack took a twenty-dollar bill from the cashbox and handed it to Alex. "We're short of ones and quarters. Take this to the Park 'n' Buy and get change, okay?"

Stuffing the twenty into her front jean pocket, Alex nodded and drew Annie aside. "Vince was *here*, Annie."

"He came to get Dad's records," Annie replied.

"He looked at me strangely!" Alex claimed in a forced whisper.

"He looks at everyone strangely," Annie said. "He's strange. But don't worry. He's gone."

"But what if he's not gone? What if he's following me?"

Annie thought about that possibility for roughly three seconds. "He's not following you. No one is following you. Believe me, Alex, if I thought you were in danger, I'd be the first one in line to protect you. But I can't protect you from yourself. It's only been twenty-one hours since you stopped using your powers, and you're becoming paranoid."

Alex glared at Annie, then realized she was shaking. "Maybe you're right. I'll try to calm down."

"You've got to." Spotting another hot prospect browsing through the knickknacks, Annie left.

Alex lapsed into troubled thought as she crossed the lawn. Nothing awful had happened all day, except in her own mind. Five-year-old brats and crabby old people were not dangerous. And her father had told Vince about the sale. Vince had stopped, bought the records, and left. Period.

It was even possible her mom really did need change, but then again, maybe she was just trying to get her out of the way for a while without hurting her feelings. Alex didn't really blame her. She couldn't seem to do anything right today.

And all because I'm not using my powers, Alex thought as she reached the sidewalk. Before she had been drenched with GC 161 and transformed into an extraordinary girl with awesome abilities, she had been convinced that she was hopelessly average and dull. Now she was sure of it.

Worse, she thought. Stripped of her powers, not only was she dismally average and dull, she couldn't get through one day without screwing up everything. Even though she had stopped the boy from cutting himself, his mother had left without spending any money. The elderly woman had snagged her own purse and tripped herself, but Alex still felt responsible. Her parents might be sued just because she had kept a box of books from falling off a table.

It was just too depressing.

CHAPTER 8

It was two-thirty and the temperature was rising steadily. Hoping to avoid a long, hot walk to the nearest convenience store, Alex stopped by Raymond's lemonade stand to see if he could break the twenty. First she plunked down a quarter and downed a cup of lemonade in one gulp, then she popped the question.

"Sorry, Alex. No can do." Raymond handed a customer a paper cup full of pink lemonade and pocketed his quarter. "I need all my change to make change."

"Business is pretty good, huh?"

"Dynamite. It's so hot, I'll clean up this afternoon . . . if I don't run out of lemonade." Raymond frowned thoughtfully.

"Why not take a break and go with me to the store? I've got to get change, and you could stock up on drink mix," Alex suggested.

"And leave this booming enterprise? No way. But wait—" Raymond reached into his pocket and pulled out a five-dollar bill. "As long as you're going, you could do me a favor and pick up a can of pink stuff."

Alex took the five and put it in her pocket with the twenty. She had to go to the store anyway, and Raymond was her best friend. "Okay. Pink stuff?"

"Pink-lemonade mix. And could you bring me my change in quarters?"

"Sure. Anything else?"

"Nope. Thanks."

Two children peddled up on plastic bicycles and put down their quarters, drawing Raymond's smiling attention.

Anxious to get to the store before the heat grew even more unbearable, Alex headed out. Normally she could walk to the Park 'n' Buy and back in half an hour, but it was too hot to hurry.

Halfway to the store Alex became uncomfortably aware that the neighborhood was mostly deserted. An occasional car went by, but the windows were always rolled up to keep the air-conditioned interiors cool. Shades were drawn to filter out the sun in all the houses. Children splashed in backyard pools here and there, but for the most part people were staying inside.

The third block was an undeveloped section of the neighborhood. Vacant lots overgrown with underbrush and scrub trees loomed on her left, and across the street, several unfinished houses stood empty.

Suddenly nervous, Alex paused to listen. Quiet prevailed. Even the neighborhood dogs were too hot to bark.

Senses alert, Alex walked faster. Once again she felt as if she was being watched. Until Vince had shown up at the yard sale, she had stopped worrying about the bizarre phone call and the black figure she had seen dart behind the Hendersons' storage shed.

Or thought she had seen.

But what if it isn't my imagination?

A clattering noise sounded on the sidewalk behind her. Alex whirled around, her heart pounding. The sidewalk was empty, but a soda can rolled off the curb and into the street.

"Who's there?"

No one answered.

Maybe because no one's there, Alex, she scolded herself.

Then she heard running footsteps.

Spinning back around, Alex stared at the spot where the sidewalk curved around a cluster of tall bushes just ahead.

The footsteps noise stopped.

Now Alex could hear nothing but her own beating heart thundering in her ears. But she was sure she'd heard footsteps. Someone was out there, trying to scare her or—worse—trying to catch her using her secret powers. Chilled in spite of the sweltering heat, Alex shuddered.

Vince.

Alex remembered the first time she had seen Vince, when he had come to their front door during the house-to-house search the day after the GC 161 accident. She recalled his hard expression, the icy-cold look in his blue eyes. He had studied her and Annie intently, wondering if one of them was the kid he was looking for.

Scared, Alex started to glow again. She did not

want to meet Vince while she was glowing. There was no way she'd be able to explain it.

Panicking, she bolted into the vacant lot and crashed through the underbrush. Her only thought was to run.

She stumbled over a rock and went down on her knees. Scrambling forward, she scraped her hands on the rough ground, then tore the hem of her T-shirt on a branch. She didn't stop until she burst through a stand of dense, dry bushes and plunged into a water-filled ditch.

Standing in water that covered her sneakers, Alex finally stopped to think. She listened to the absence of noise.

No twigs snapped.

No leaves rustled.

No one was chasing her.

"Dork. Jerk. Geek." Mumbling, Alex climbed out of the ditch. She was a mess. Her arms were criss-crossed with red scratches, and her jeans were streaked with dirt. Her torn T-shirt was splattered with mud, and her sneakers and socks were soggy.

Her imagination had gotten the best of her again, and she was mad.

Angling back toward the street, Alex listened

to her shoes squish and fumed about just how reckless and stupid her panicked flight had been. She should have run toward the populated section of the neighborhood—not into a vacant lot where there was no one around to help. Besides, dare or no dare, she could use her powers to save herself if she was really in danger. What really bothered her was that because she had those powers, she *had* forgotten how to think her way out of problem situations.

How would she do without them for real—if she were ever forced to?

Alex stomped toward the Park 'n' Buy another block away. She'd forgotten about the heat and her dirty clothes. All she could think about was how she had *not* stopped to think.

Since Annie's twenty-four-hour dare, Alex had wanted to prove to herself as well as Annie that she could function without using her special abilities. Now it was more than a matter of self-respect.

It was a matter of survival.

This time the danger was only a figment of her imagination, but sooner or later she would find herself in a dangerous situation that wouldn't allow her to use her powers safely.

Alex made a promise to herself as she marched across the street to the convenience store. From now on she would use her brains to solve her problems, just like everyone else.

"Hey, Ben," Alex said as she walked inside. Ben was in high school and worked at the store every Saturday afternoon. He was always friendly, and Alex liked to talk with him when she came in. Not today. Bedraggled and dirty, she knew she was a pathetic sight. She just hoped Ben had the courtesy not to mention it.

Alex grabbed a large can of pink drink mix for Raymond, then strolled up to the counter.

"This it?" Ben asked.

"Yeah, and change for a twenty. Ones and quarters, if you've got them to spare."

"No problem. Heard you were having a yard sale."

Nodding, Alex reached into her pocket, then stiffened. She drove her hand in deeper, all the way to the seam. It couldn't be! Her mom's twenty and Raymond's five were gone!

"Uh—on second thought maybe I'd better come back later. See ya!"

Leaving the drink mix on the counter, Alex rushed outside. Twenty-five dollars—gone. And it wasn't even her money! *Worse than dumb*, she raged at herself. Losing the bills was completely and totally irresponsible.

Certain the twenty and five had fallen out of her pocket while she was dashing panic-stricken through the vacant lot, Alex decided to go look for them. It might take a while to find them, but getting back late would be infinitely better than going home with no drink mix and no change. Raymond had trusted her with his profits, and her mother had only wanted her to feel useful.

As Alex started back across the street, the pay phone by the convenience store rang. She stopped and looked around. No one was waiting by the phone for someone to return his call.

It rang again.

Alex pushed open the front door and hollered to Ben. "The phone's ringing out here!"

Ben just shrugged. "It's not our phone. Probably a wrong number. Happens all the time."

The phone rang again and then again.

Alex hesitated, then gave into her curiosity and answered it on the fifth ring. "Hello?"

A loud whistling sound rang in Alex's ears.

It was the same sound she had heard on the kitchen phone that morning!

CHAPTER 9

Alex hung up the phone and wheeled to scan up and down the street.

No one in sight—again.

But someone was definitely out there, and that someone was definitely watching and following her. Alex didn't doubt that for a minute—not anymore. She had not imagined the whistling phone calls. Both calls were real, and both had been intended for her! Getting the second call on a pay phone outside the Park 'n' Buy was just too bizarre to be a coincidence.

The watcher must have gotten the number

when she was inside and then called from another pay phone nearby. *Maybe from the gas station on the next block,* Alex thought nervously. Nothing else explained it.

Alex darted across the street and ran toward home.

Whether someone was playing a cruel game or had more sinister motives, one thing was certain. He—or she—did not want to be seen or identified. If Vince was the watcher, he obviously didn't have enough evidence to make a move. Why anyone else would want to terrorize her was a complete mystery.

Rhonda Clark had good reason to dislike her, but she had been at home last night when Alex had seen someone looking through the kitchen window.

Legs pounding the pavement, Alex sprinted past the vacant lot. She didn't dare stop to look for the lost money. Whoever was following her might suddenly decide it was time to do more than just watch and make phone calls. Although her powers could save her, she was determined to make the right decisions and rely on herself to do what had to be done. Going directly home was the smartest thing to do.

Jogging the last two blocks, Alex finally arrived safe and sound. Breathless, dirty, and scared, she ran past Raymond's lemonade stand.

"Hey, Alex!" Raymond called. "Did ya get my drink stuff?"

"Later, Raymond!"

"And my change?"

"Not now, Raymond!"

Alex didn't slow down until she reached the tree where her father was still playing cashier. Even though it was midafternoon and broiling hot, there were more people in the yard now than there had been that morning. Alex leaned against the tree to catch her breath.

"There you are, Alex." Mr. Mack handed a woman a computer-printed receipt, then cast a quick glance at Alex. "You've been gone a long time, sweetheart. I ran out of quarters fifteen minutes ago."

"Dad, there's something I've got to tell—"

Mrs. Mack walked by, then paused to look back. Noting Alex's tattered appearance, she frowned with concern. "Where have you been? You've been gone over an hour."

"That's what I've been trying to—"

"Oh, for real, Alex!" Annie stood off a few feet,

shaking her head, then turned to her mother. "I'm going upstairs to find my old suede boots, Mom. I think I'll sell them."

"Okay, dear," Mrs. Mack said absently. Her attention was still on Alex.

"I could use those quarters now, Alex." Mr. Mack didn't look at her, but continued to total up another customer's purchases on his computer. As usual, he was oblivious to everything except what he was working on. He hadn't even noticed that she looked like the loser in a tug-of-war over a mud pit. It wasn't that he didn't care. George Mack was just incredibly single-minded.

"I don't have them," Alex muttered.

"The Park 'n' Buy wouldn't give you change?" Mrs. Mack asked in disbelief.

"No, I—I lost the twenty when—"

Mr. Mack's head snapped around. "You *lost* twenty dollars!"

"Alex, how could you be so careless?" Mrs. Mack exhaled in exasperation. "You know how hard we've worked for that money."

"Yes, but—"

"How could you lose a twenty-dollar bill between here and a store that's only four blocks away?" Mrs. Mack asked sternly.

"It wasn't my fault! I—"

"No excuses, Alex!" Mrs. Mack snapped. "You simply have to learn to be more careful."

"Someone was following me, Mom!" Alex said in desperation. "I lost it when I ran away!"

"Who was following you?" Mrs. Mack pressed.

Alex hesitated. "I don't know. I didn't actually *see* anyone, but there was this phone call, and—"

"Everyone makes mistakes, Alex. You don't have to make up stories to—yes?" A smile replaced the frown on Mrs. Mack's face when a well-dressed woman tapped her on the shoulder.

"I could use some help over here," the woman said pleasantly.

"Of course." Mrs. Mack took off behind the woman, but not before frowning once again in Alex's direction.

"I'm not making up excuses," Alex said defensively, but her mother was already halfway across the yard and didn't hear. She turned to her father. "Dad?"

Mr. Mack shook his head. "Your mother's right, Alex. You have to learn to be more responsible." A slow frown wrinkled his brow. "Go change your clothes. You're a mess."

"Right."

Hanging her head, Alex shuffled into the house. Her parents didn't believe that she was being followed and harassed by an unknown person for unknown reasons. That was almost more upsetting than being followed. For all she knew, some weird lunatic had targeted her for *no* logical reason. Even though nothing like that had ever happened in Paradise Valley, stranger things happened all the time in other places.

It would serve everyone right if something terrible did happen to her. Then maybe they'd be convinced she wasn't imagining things or lying.

Angry and feeling rejected, Alex slammed the front door behind her and ran up the stairs. Annie was kneeling in front of their closet, throwing shoes and clothes over her shoulder.

"Where *are* they?" Annie asked herself.

"What?" Alex answered as she flopped on her bed.

"My suede boots. They're worth twenty bucks to some old hippie lady outside."

"They're not worth anything if you can't find them." Alex kicked off her wet sneakers and peeled off her soggy socks.

"Very funny." Sitting back on her heels, Annie glowered at Alex over her shoulder. "I'd be able to find them if your half of the closet wasn't such a mess. Have you seen them?''

''Maybe.'' Alex stood up and shrugged. ''Then again, maybe I just *imagined* I saw them under my red cap in the right-hand corner of the top shelf.''

Annie jumped up and tripped on a shoe as she stepped toward the shelf. She fell against the closet door, banging it into a floor lamp in the corner. The slanted slats in the door rattled, and bits of paint rained down from where the lamp hit the wall.

Alex noticed, but ignored it. She was still angry at everyone for not believing her story, but she was more angry with Annie. Her parents didn't know she had strange powers that someone might want to expose or exploit. Annie did.

Kicking clothes and shoes out of the way, Annie stood on tiptoe and strained to reach her boots.

''I could make it easy for you and levitate them off the shelf, Annie, but it's only three-fifteen. No powers for another two hours. Sorry.''

Snagging the boots, Annie dragged them down and turned to regard Alex with genuine worry. ''What's wrong with you all of a sudden, Alex?''

''With me?'' Alex's eyes widened in mock surprise. ''Nothing much. I'm being followed by some nut who dresses in black and peers in windows, and I'm getting weird, whistling phone calls on pay phones. No one believes me, but other than that there's nothing's wrong with me!" Alex paused to get her breath.

"Well, I've got to give you credit for one thing," Annie said as she walked to the door. "Your mind may be overcompensating because you feel deprived of your powers, but at least you're not using them."

"I'm not imagining things!" Alex yelled as Annie ran down the hall to the stairs.

Alone and even angrier, Alex yanked off her jeans and went to the closet for a clean pair. In a fit of temper, she pushed the door hard, slamming it against the lamp and the wall. As she entered, the door rebounded off the wall and banged closed, shutting her inside.

Then she heard a loud crash. The floor lamp had fallen over.

"Great." Alex reached for the doorknob. The knob turned in her hand, but the door wouldn't open. She pushed against it. The door held fast.

Stuck? How?

The slats slanted downward, and through them Alex could see a gold metal rod angled across the door. The lamp had fallen in front of the door and must have become wedged between the wall and the dresser beside the closet.

Trapped.

Alex tugged on the light cord dangling in front of her face. The lightbulb sputtered and sparked, then blew out in a brief flash of light.

Trapped in the dark.

Angry, frightened, and frustrated, Alex exploded. This had been absolutely the worst day of her life, and all because Annie had conned her into not using her powers. She was being terrorized by someone, and her parents didn't care enough even to listen! And now she was locked in a stupid closet!

As bad as it was, she was determined not to use her powers.

Fighting back tears, Alex lashed out at the door. She threw herself against it, shaking the frame, but it remained stuck. She threw her weight against it again. One of the slats cracked. She hit the slat with her fist, and it broke. With another angry blow, she broke the one above it, creating an opening just wide enough for her hand.

Reaching through the break, Alex grabbed the metal pole and pushed up on it. The flimsy metal bent, but the end was dislodged from behind the dresser. Broken glass from the shattered globe clinked on the floor as Alex lifted the pole and opened the closet door. Her anger spent, Alex took a deep breath, then stepped out.

Rummaging through the pile of clothes Annie had left in a heap on the floor, Alex found clean shorts and a tank-top. After washing up, she changed. Then, too emotionally and physically drained to do anything else for a while, she sat down on her bed to stare out the window.

She wasn't angry anymore or even pleased because she had freed herself from the closet without using her powers. She was just plain worn out and scared.

Someone was watching. . . .

When the phone rang, she didn't answer.

CHAPTER 10

When the phone rang again half an hour later, Alex was still in bed, staring at the ceiling. She heard the message on the answering machine in her parents' bedroom.

"Hey, Alex. It's Nicole. Call me when you can, okay?"

Alex hurried into her parents' bedroom and picked up.

"Hi, Nicole. What's up?" Alex asked without much enthusiasm.

"Nothing much. Robyn's here, and we thought

you might want to come over later, after the yard sale's over."

"I don't know. I'll have to see."

"Are you all right, Alex? You sound really down."

"I'm fine. Just tired. Call ya later."

After hanging up, Alex rose and went back to her own room. She was tired—but too tired to see her friends? A spark of anger jolted her out of the funk she had fallen into. Hiding in her bedroom and feeling sorry for herself wouldn't solve anything. She had to figure out who was harassing her and why, and then do something about it.

Without using my powers, Alex resolved. *I got along fine for thirteen years before GC 161 changed my life. I can do this.*

It was now after four, but the late afternoon sun was still sizzling. Alex looked down into the yard as she started to close the blinds.

Below, the crowd was beginning to thin. Last-minute bargains were being struck with Annie and her mother, and her father was asking departing customers if they could change the bills clutched in his hand.

When she saw Annie dismantling a card table, Alex felt a twinge of guilt. She hadn't done much to help out today, even if it was sort of justified. *I should go down and start putting things away,* she thought as she tied her sneakers.

Alex was startled by the sudden sound of tires squealing around a corner. She glanced out the window and saw an old blue Mustang convertible roar down the street. It didn't slow as it zoomed past the house and barely missed hitting a man crossing the street. Furious, her father yelled at the speeding car.

Alex frowned, trying to remember why the car looked so familiar. Even though the top was down, the Mustang had gone by too fast to see the young couple inside clearly.

At the next corner the car screeched to a stop. Then the driver made a U-turn and drove slowly back, giving her a chance to see who was in the car.

Alex swallowed hard. It was Mike Warner and Meg Halsey!

She hesitated for a brief, tense moment. Why hadn't she thought of them before? They had been seriously ticked off when the security guard threw them out of the department store. Even though Mike had accused Rhonda of shoving the carts at him, he thought she and Rhonda were together. Were Mike and Meg following her and making those weird phone calls to get even? They were notorious troublemakers, and it made perfect sense. They might even be harassing Rhonda, too.

Alex dashed out of her room and down the stairs to the front door. "Now's my chance," she said to herself. "I'm not going to stand by and do nothing." Mike and Meg were just kids. Older and bigger than she, and rowdier than most kids, but just kids. She had to stand up to them and show them she couldn't be intimidated by their scare tactics. Then maybe they'd stop. If they knew she wasn't afraid, scaring her wouldn't be fun anymore.

Throwing open the front door, Alex ran outside. The blue Mustang was parked on the far side of the street, and Mike and Meg were climbing out. Her father marched toward them, waving them back.

"You two just keep on going!" Mr. Mack shouted. "This is a residential street, not a racetrack!"

"Yeah, yeah." Mike draped his arm over Meg's shoulder. "We just want to take a look at your stuff."

"You almost hit that man over there!"

Alex hurried across the lawn, wondering if Mike might suddenly decide to throw a punch at her dad.

"Cool your jets, old man," Mike jeered. "Nobody got hurt."

"Get lost!" Mr. Mack demanded.

"Who's gonna make us?" Meg glared.

Alex had never seen her father so angry. Squaring his shoulders, he advanced toward the car. The man Mike had almost run down fell into step beside him.

Apparently Mike decided that a yard sale wasn't worth the hassle of provoking a fight with her furious father and the angry stranger. He and Meg spun around and hopped back into his car.

And then Mike saw her.

Alex stopped at the curb and met Mike's hostile stare. His eyes narrowed with recognition and his mouth tightened as he shoved the car into gear, then sped away with another scream of rubber.

Alex watched the Mustang disappear with mixed feelings of relief and dread. She was thrilled her father had stood his ground and chased them off, but he had also given them more reason to keep harassing her. They might not be satisfied with just following and calling her now—if Mike and Meg were guilty, which seemed pretty likely.

Without her powers Alex knew she'd get the worst of it if they decided to pick a real fight. How would she cope if she couldn't zap, morph, or move things with her thoughts?

Get help, Alex decided. *But who?*Not her parents . . . not yet. This was strictly between kids.

Alex's gaze drifted over to Raymond on his front lawn. Collecting an empty pitcher and his unused paper cups, he went into his house. It looked as if Raymond was out of lemonade and out of business because she had lost his money. Alex sighed. He'd help if she asked, but she decided to wait until she had exhausted all her other options. Now all she had to do was figure out who else would want to get tangled up with the likes of Mike and Meg. Who else had it in for those two teen terrors? And then it came to Alex in a flash: Rhonda Clark, that's who!

Alex rushed inside to get Rhonda's phone number. If Rhonda was being followed and getting whistling phone calls, too, then Alex would know for sure that Mike and Meg were responsible. And maybe Rhonda would even agree to help her. Alex dialed, and Rhonda answered on the first ring.

"Hello?"

"Rhonda. Hi. This is Alex—"

Rhonda hung up.

"Mack . . ." Alex finished, then pushed the disconnect button. Should she try again? Rhonda might still be worried that she would tell someone about the attempted shoplifting. *Or*, Alex thought with a gasp, *if Rhonda is getting whistling phone calls, maybe she thinks I'm making them!*

Alex dialed again. The phone rang and rang, but Rhonda didn't answer. Alex was not totally surprised. She had stopped answering the phone, too.

"Hey, Alex." Annie stood in the doorway between the kitchen and the living room with her hands on her hips. "Mom's decided to close up shop. You gonna help or what?"

"Sure." Alex hung up the receiver. It rang, and she jumped back with a startled yelp. It rang a second and third time before Annie realized she wasn't going to answer it.

Alex tensed as Annie sprang across the room and dived for the phone. If Annie heard the whistle, then she'd finally believe her story.

"Hello?" Annie paused. "Oh, hi, Mr. Cummings."

Alex's shoulders sagged. Mr. Cummings worked with her father, and they often got together on weekends to discuss particularly interesting or difficult projects.

"Sure, I'll tell him. No need to call you back ... okay. Got it. Bye."

Hanging up, Annie turned to Alex. "Now I *know* something's wrong with you, Al. Since when don't you answer the phone?"

"Since this afternoon," Alex stated calmly. "Someone called this morning and blew a whistle in my ear! Then it happened again at the pay phone outside the Park 'n' Buy."

"Really?" Annie frowned. "That's strange, all right. Why didn't you say something?"

"I tried, but no one would listen." Alex was so grateful that Annie was finally paying attention, she couldn't stay angry. "And I'm absolutely positive that—"

"Annie!" Mrs. Mack shouted from the front door. "Alex! Come on. I want to get all this stuff out of the yard before dark."

"It's only four-thirty, Mom!" Annie called back.

"Now, please!"

"Guess we'd better go help." Annie paused in the doorway. "You can fill me in later, after I beg your forgiveness and apologize."

"Apologize? For what?"

Annie grinned sheepishly. "I didn't think you could do it, Alex. Go for a whole day without using your powers, I mean."

Alex grinned back. "How do you know I didn't?"

"Get real, Alex. Nothing's gone right for you today, not even walking a few blocks to get change. You didn't use them."

"No, I didn't, but you were right, though," Alex admitted solemnly. "I was relying on them too much."

"Well, that's something." A sparkle brightened Annie's brown eyes as she glanced at the clock. "But there's still forty-five minutes to go. It's not over yet."

"Forty-three," Alex quipped, then laughed as she followed Annie into the yard.

While Annie and Mrs. Mack sorted and boxed the household and hardware items, Alex folded clothes. Even though they had sold a ton of junk, there was still a lot to put away.

"George!" Mrs. Mack tugged on a cardboard

box full of tools. It was too heavy for her to lift alone. "Can you help me with this?"

"Two hundred and fifty-two dollars and forty cents." Mr. Mack stood up and shut off his laptop computer. He folded it closed and handed it to Annie to take inside. "Not bad, gang. Not bad at all."

Alex was impressed, although she wished she had been more help.

"Take the cashbox inside, will you, Alex?" Mr. Mack asked.

"Right away, Dad." Alex headed for the tree while her father hurried over to help her mother. Even working together, her parents couldn't lift the box. They dragged it toward the garage.

"Yo, Alex!" Raymond hollered from the sidewalk where he was taking down his lemonade stand.

Alex stopped and turned slowly. She had forgotten about Raymond's five dollars, which made her feel worse than she already did. "Hi, Raymond."

"Got a minute?"

"Yeah." Bracing herself, Alex walked over to join him. Putting off telling him she had lost his money wouldn't make the job any easier. *Might as well get it over with.*

"Are you okay, Alex?" A worried frown settled over Raymond's usually cheerful face.

Alex just looked at him a moment. She had expected him to be upset because she had lost his money and hadn't gotten his drink mix. But instead he was worried about her.

"I'm fine, but there's something I've got to—"

"Hey!" Raymond's head jerked up, his eyes looking past her. "What are you doing?"

Alex turned to see a girl dressed in black standing by her father's table under the tree. Long, blond hair fanned out behind her as the girl whirled to face them.

Rhonda?

Alex couldn't believe her eyes. She had just talked to Rhonda on the phone. The girl couldn't possibly have gotten here from her house in twenty minutes.

Then Alex noticed the cellular phone dangling from the girl's belt.

A mobile phone! That explained everything.

"I have to talk to you!" Alex called out and started across the lawn.

But Rhonda had other ideas.

Grabbing the cashbox, she took off running through the Hendersons' front yard.

It took a moment for Alex to register what Rhonda was really up to. She saw Rhonda tuck the cashbox under her arm and realized that the girl was doing it again—stealing!

"Stop!" Alex cried out. "You can't get away with this!"

CHAPTER 11

"She's stealing your cashbox!" Raymond said in shocked surprise.

But Alex had already taken off after Rhonda, passing her father as she streaked across the driveway.

"Alex? Where are you going?" Mr. Mack asked.

Blocked by a thick hedge, Rhonda turned and ran behind the Hendersons' house.

Alex kept running. Behind her she heard Raymond trying to explain the situation to her father. "Rhonda Clark just ran off with your money, Mr. Mack! And yesterday Alex caught her trying to shoplift a pair of earrings. Maybe you'd better call the police or something.''

"No, I've got a better idea," Mr. Mack said.

Alex bolted around the side of the Hendersons' house and didn't hear the rest of the conversation. Ahead of her, Rhonda swerved to avoid a wheelbarrow, stumbled, then darted out of sight behind the storage shed.

Rhonda knew exactly where she was going, Alex realized. The girl had disappeared behind the Hendersons' shed that very morning.

Suddenly all the pieces fell into place. When Alex had called Rhonda last night and twenty minutes ago, the kleptomaniac had not been home on the far side of town. Rhonda had been nearby, answering her cellular phone. There were numerous places she could have hidden and watched when Alex went into the Park 'n' Buy. Then she had called the pay phone from her mobile phone when Alex came out of the store.

Ducking through a break in the hedge that lined the back of the Hendersons' yard, Alex paused. A flash of black zipping between two houses caught her eye, and she gave chase again.

Alex had to catch Rhonda, and for more reasons than just getting the yard-sale money back. Her father had asked her to take the cashbox into the house, had *trusted* her to take charge of the money even though she had messed up one thing after another all day long. Leaving the cashbox unattended was just one more screwup, but it was one she intended to set right.

Hitting the sidewalk, Alex saw Rhonda cut across a yard on the corner. Alex did not break stride. She ran faster, hoping to cut the distance between herself and the fleeing girl.

It would be so easy to use my powers now, Alex thought as she rounded the corner. Rhonda was only half a block away. If Alex wanted to, she could simply reach out with a thought and snatch the cashbox right out of Rhonda's hands. But Alex was determined not to resort to telekinesis.

Besides, Alex had to know *why* Rhonda Clark had embarked on a crime spree of shoplifting, stalking, and robbery.

And almost as important, why had the girl singled out Alex as a target? Alex hadn't done anything but try to save Rhonda from making a big mistake that could have ruined her life.

Rhonda looked back over her shoulder, then dashed across the street and into another yard.

Alex shaved off more distance by cutting across

the street at an angle. She was gasping for air when she entered the yard, but she kept going. Rhonda had to be winded, too. Sooner or later Alex would catch up. She wasn't going to give up.

Concentrating on breathing and keeping her legs moving, Alex followed Rhonda into another yard and across another street. Steadily gaining ground, Alex was only ten yards behind the girl when Rhonda turned onto a narrow back street. It ran between a long row of apartment buildings on one side and behind the shops and stores that lined the main avenue.

As Alex turned to pursue the girl, she heard an engine roar on the side street behind her. She looked back, but the car was already out of sight behind Murphy's Variety Store.

Just ahead, Rhonda paused in confusion, then suddenly zigged to the left and ran up an alley between two apartment buildings.

Her lungs burning from the effort, Alex turned left and came to an abrupt halt. Rhonda was doubled over, gasping in front of a cement wall that prevented traffic from using the driveway as a through street. She had reached a dead end with no way out. The chase was over.

A couple of tense and silent minutes passed as

both girls fought to catch their breath. Rhonda spoke first.

"Okay, Alex. You caught me. Now what are you going to do about it?" Rhonda's expression was openly hostile and challenging. She still clutched the cashbox under her arm.

"That depends." Alex inhaled and walked slowly forward.

"Depends on what?" Rhonda laughed. "You know I tried to shoplift those earrings, and you just caught me stealing your family's yard-sale money. Why not just call the cops?"

Alex studied Rhonda. Although the girl had been laughing, her eyes looked sad. Rhonda didn't seem like the coolest girl in school anymore.

"How come you've been watching me and making those phone calls?" Alex asked bluntly.

Rhonda just looked at the ground.

"You wanted to get caught stealing, Rhonda," Alex said softly. "Why?"

"It doesn't really matter, does it?"

"It does to me," Alex said honestly. She sensed that Rhonda was upset about something, and she wanted to help. "I mean, you've got everything anyone could possibly want. You're popular and smart. So why blow it all for a cheap thrill?"

"What do you know about anything?" Rhonda's eyes flashed with sudden anger. "You're the one who's got it made—not me!"

"Me?" Alex stared in amazement at the pretty blond girl for a moment. "Get real! Most of the kids in school don't even know my name! I'm a boring, ordinary nobody!"

"Your parents don't think so!" A tear formed in Rhonda's eye and rolled slowly down her cheek.

"My parents?" Alex started, genuinely puzzled.

"Yes. I've been watching you," Rhonda admitted. "Last night and all day today. You've made one stupid mistake after another, but your parents don't care that you can't do anything right."

That's the truth, Alex thought, *but why does it matter so much to Rhonda?*

"I get straight A's!" Rhonda went on. "I get elected to the student council and land the lead in the school play. And the biggest reaction I get from my parents is a nod or maybe a smile, when they notice at all. If *my* mom had a yard sale, she'd send me to the movies to keep me out of the way!"

"It can't be that bad, Rhonda."

Tears rolled freely down Rhonda's cheeks. "When they're not working at the plant, they're playing golf or making contacts at the country club. They don't have time for me."

"So that's why you started stealing things?"

Rhonda blinked, sniffling. "Mmm . . ."

Alex was beginning to see things clearly now. Rhonda might not realize it, but she had resorted to stealing as a way to get her parents' attention. She had tried and succeeded in being the perfect child, but her parents still ignored her. So Rhonda started getting into trouble—a desperate way to force them to notice her.

"Think about it, Rhonda," Alex said. "What would happen if your parents found out you were shoplifting?"

"I don't know what you're talking about." Wiping her eyes, Rhonda fixed Alex with a defiant glare.

"If you got arrested, they'd have to drop everything to handle the problem, wouldn't they?"

Rhonda hesitated, then sagged. "Yeah. I guess they would."

Alex felt really sorry for Rhonda, especially when she realized how interested her own parents were in her and Annie. Considering Rhonda's situation, she also felt bad for being angry at her mom for not believing her earlier. Her mom's reaction was understandable under the circumstances. Alex *had* lost the money, and her story about being followed had sounded like an excuse.

And even though her father was often preoccupied, he always listened once she got his attention.

"Rhonda, there's got to be a better way to solve your problem. Stealing just doesn't cut it, you know?"

Rhonda sighed, then nodded. "I suppose you're right."

"Being a hopeless screwup isn't the answer, either," Alex added for good measure. "Believe me. I know."

A warm smile brightened Rhonda's somber face. "You're not a *hopeless* screwup, Alex. I was watching, remember?"

"Oh, yeah? And what did you see?"

"Most of that stuff that went wrong wasn't your fault." Rhonda hesitated thoughtfully. "You're actually very cool, Alex. You could have turned me in for trying to take those earrings, but you didn't. Thanks."

Alex shrugged self-consciously. "Just promise

me you won't try anything that dumb again. Or blow whistles through the phone!"

"Promise." Rhonda dug into her pants pocket and pulled out two bills—a twenty and a five. "These are yours. I picked them up in the vacant lot after they fell out of your pocket. And this, too." She held out the bills and the cashbox.

"We'll take those!" a hard, male voice barked.

Rhonda's eyes widened with fear.

Alex snapped her head around. Meg and Mike stood directly behind her, blocking the drive.

CHAPTER 12

"What do you want?" Alex stepped back to stand beside Rhonda, but she didn't take her eyes off Mike and Meg.

"Those bills," Meg said evenly.

"And the cashbox." Mike's angry gaze fastened on Alex.

Rhonda paled and started to shake.

"What cashbox?" Alex asked, stalling for time to think.

Mike's eyes narrowed and his jaw flexed. "Give it up, kid. You guys have caused me and Meg a bunch of trouble lately, and now you're gonna pay. Got it?"

"Yeah." Meg moved in beside Mike. "Running people down with shopping carts and getting them thrown out of stores ain't cool."

Mike glowered at Rhonda. "I don't know how you hit me with that cart, but nobody messes with me like that and gets away with it."

Rhonda just shook her head. She was too terrified to talk.

"That was an accident." Alex struggled to control the tremor in her voice. "We didn't try to hurt you on purpose."

"Your old man thinks he's too good for us, chasing us off a public street—on purpose." Meg glared at Alex defiantly.

"It wasn't a total loss, though." Meg put a smug smile on her face. "We found both of you. Chasin' you guys has been a blast, but the fun's over. Give us the money."

"And maybe we'll go easy on you," Mike added.

Alex's mind went into high gear as she sized up the situation. She didn't dare use her powers. Mike was already suspicious because of the scene at the store with the shopping carts, and Rhonda knew she hadn't done it herself. Alex simply couldn't risk it.

Besides, even though the twenty-four-hour dare was almost over, not using her powers had become a matter of personal pride. Alex had to get out of this without them.

Think, Alex! Meg and Mike were blocking the only escape route. Somehow, she had to distract them so she and Rhonda could make a break for it. But first she had to snap Rhonda out of her petrified daze.

Alex poked Rhonda in the side.

Rhonda didn't even flinch. She just stared at Mike and Meg as if she were in a trance.

Then Alex realized she was getting more tense and nervous. *What if I start to glow now?* The fear of being found out made her even more nervous. She had to distract herself, too.

Alex laughed and poked Rhonda again.

Rhonda jumped slightly.

Mike and Meg exchanged glances, then Meg scowled. "What's so funny?"

Still laughing, Alex chanced a glance at the frightened girl beside her. Then she noticed the cellular phone clipped to her belt. An outrageous idea burst into Alex's head. Rhonda had called her house less than an hour ago. If she pushed the redial button, someone at home would answer. It was a long shot, but if she could get Rhonda's attention and keep Mike and Meg off guard, it might work.

Alex began moving her hand as though she were dribbling an invisible basketball, then danced in front of Rhonda.

"Wanna play, Rhonda?"

Rhonda blinked and looked Alex directly in the eye.

"Might as well play 'cause we can't *call for help.*" Alex shifted her gaze to the little cellular phone, then back to Rhonda. Rhonda's eyes widened a little. *Did she get the message?* Alex could only hope.

Still pretending to dribble, Alex bounced around to face Mike and Meg. "Somebody called *my house,*" Alex chanted. "Somebody *called again!*"

Mike sighed, looking bored. "Acting like a dork isn't gonna save you, you know."

"But she's so entertaining!" Meg laughed sarcastically, but she didn't move. Both bullies seemed willing to let Alex make a fool of herself for a little while longer.

"Catch a *clue,* we're on to you!" Alex whirled toward Rhonda.

Rhonda inclined her head and moved her hand toward the phone.

Mike and Meg were ignoring Rhonda and watching Alex.

Trusting the girl to push the redial button without giving the plan away, Alex leaped and threw the invisible ball toward an invisible basket.

"Missed!" Alex pretended to catch the make-believe ball and cast another glance at Rhonda.

Rhonda smiled.

Yes! Rhonda had taken the cue and pushed redial. At home someone would answer and be able to hear what was going on through the open line. If Alex could feed them the right information, they'd come to help.

Dribbling again, Alex wheeled back around to confront Mike and Meg again. "So—you two want the cash box, huh? Want to fight for it here? Behind Jody's Café? Two big guys against two little guys who just want to forget it and go home?"

Both bullies were too fascinated by Alex's antics to realize what she was doing. They were, however, losing patience.

"Whenever you're ready, you little dweeb." Meg took a threatening step forward.

Alex and Rhonda were running out of time.

"I'd rather play something else," Rhonda said. Stuffing the bills back in her pocket, Rhonda started a pretend game of her own. Holding the cashbox like a football, she dropped into a hike position. "Twenty-two! Forty-eight!"

Alex clued into Rhonda's plan immediately.

"Hut!"

When Rhonda tossed Alex the cashbox, she caught it, tucked it under her arm, and ran.

Confused by Rhonda's unexpected move, Meg and Mike hesitated. Alex charged between them, knocking Meg off balance as she passed. Rhonda ducked around Mike, and both girls took off like a couple of running backs.

"Get them!" Mike yelled.

Alex looked behind her shoulder to see Mike and Meg charging after them. Older and bigger, the two outraged teenagers would catch her and Rhonda before they reached the street.

Then Alex heard Annie call her name.

"Alex! Where are you?"

"Alex!" Raymond yelled.

Mike slowed down and Meg tumbled into him.

Alex and Rhonda dashed out the driveway, around the apartment security wall, and right past Annie, Raymond, Robyn, and Nicole.

"Whoa there!" Annie shouted.

Alex skidded to a halt and turned just as Mike and Meg emerged from the drive. They stopped, saw six kids instead of two, then bolted in the opposite direction.

"Annie! Raymond! Boy, am I glad to see you!" Alex exclaimed breathlessly.

"A cellular phone," Annie said with a glance at Rhonda. "I wondered how you managed to call. Pretty ingenious."

Rhonda smiled. "It was Alex's great idea."

"Way to go!" Raymond agreed. "When Annie answered the phone and heard what was going on, we didn't have any trouble figuring out where you were. That was brilliant!"

"Are you all right?" Nicole asked anxiously.

"Fine," Alex panted. She shifted her curious gaze between Robyn and Nicole. "What are you doing here?"

Robyn answered. "Nicole said you sounded kinda bummed on the phone, so we came over to cheer you up."

"And joined the posse as we ran out the door," Raymond explained. "Guess we got here in the nick of time, too, huh?"

"Yeah. I just hope they don't come back." Alex looked in the direction Mike and Meg had taken.

"They won't," Nicole said. "It's six against two. Bullies don't like those kinds of odds."

"Rhonda!" a man called.

Alex turned and saw her father and another man hurrying down the street toward them.

"Dad!" Rhonda gasped.

Mr. Clark stopped in front of Rhonda and gripped her by the shoulders. "Are you hurt?"

Rhonda shook her head. "No. Thanks to Alex, I'm okay." She paused, obviously bewildered. "What are you doing here, Dad?"

"Mr. Mack called me," Rhonda's father said sternly. "Right after you stole his cashbox."

Annie motioned to Raymond, Robyn, and Nicole. "Everything seems to be under control here, so we're gonna go, Dad. See you at home."

"Why are we leaving?" Raymond asked as Annie drew him away.

"Because this is none of our business, Ray."

"Right," Robyn said, taking the hint and tugging on Nicole's sleeve. "See you when you get back to the house, Alex."

Alex hung back as her friends left. There was one thing she had to say to Rhonda's father. "She didn't exactly steal the cashbox, Mr. Clark.'' Alex patted the metal box tucked under her arm. "I've got it.''

"Nice try, Alex, but"—Rhonda paused with a shaky sigh—"I did steal it.''

"Why?'' Mr. Clark asked, bewildered.

Rhonda hung her head. "Just—because.''

"Because?'' Mr. Clark looked completely baffled. "But you must have had a reason, Rhonda.''

Rhonda sighed and just shook her head.

"Tell him, Rhonda,'' Alex whispered in the girl's ear. "You don't have anything to lose, right?''

"Yeah, guess not.'' Rhonda inhaled deeply. "I'm sorry, Dad. I thought that if I got into real trouble, maybe you'd pay more attention to me.'' She exhaled and looked hesitantly into her father's eyes.

"I had no idea you felt that way, honey.'' Mr. Clark studied Rhonda with a concerned expression. He didn't seem to know what to say next.

Mr. Mack cleared his throat. "Maybe you two had better go on home and have a nice, long talk.''

"But Rhonda took your money, Mr. Mack. We can't—''

Mr. Mack waved Mr. Clark's concern aside. "Alex has the cashbox now, and I don't think this is something Rhonda's going to try again. Right?''

"Never." Rhonda leaned against her father as he put a protective arm around her and led her away. Suddenly she pulled free and ran back. After digging the two lost bills out of her pocket again, Rhonda handed them to Alex.

"Catch ya Monday, Alex. I'll tell you all about getting your ears pierced at lunch, okay?"

"Okay." Alex grinned and waved as Rhonda left with her father. Alex wasn't at all sure she still wanted to get her ears pierced, but that wasn't important. Rhonda was making a gesture of friendship, and no one could have enough good friends.

"Well . . ." Mr. Mack smiled. "We'd better get home, too."

Alex felt so good about everything that she started skipping her way home. Not only had she gone twenty-four hours without using her powers, she had managed to think her way out of a serious situation. She couldn't wait to give Annie a big thank-you for pointing out that she depended on her unique abilities too much. After all that had happened, she now knew that she could depend on herself when she had to.

And thanks to Rhonda, Alex realized just how lucky she was to have parents that really cared and took an active interest in her.

"Hey, Dad. Why don't we watch a video after we get done putting the yard-sale stuff away?"

Mr. Mack didn't answer.

Alex glanced at her father. Deep in thought, he hadn't heard her. He walked with his hands stuffed in his pockets and his eyes on the sky.

"Annie's building a spaceship in the garage, and I'm going to be the pilot."

"That's nice," Mr. Mack mumbled.

Alex stifled a giggle. Although it was sometimes impossible to get her father's attention, he was *always* there when she needed him. She didn't know what great thoughts he was thinking, but for now she was content to just walk by his side.

They turned a corner and Alex spied a tricycle parked in the middle of the sidewalk. Mr. Mack was still watching the sky, unaware of everything around him.

"Dad?"

Nothing.

Alex shrugged and engaged her telekinetic power. The tricycle rolled out of the way before her father tripped over it. She had already proved to herself that she didn't *need* her powers, but it couldn't hurt to stay in practice.

ABOUT THE AUTHOR

Diana G. Gallagher lives in California with her daughter, Chelsea, her best friend, Betsey, three dogs, and five cats. Her grown son, Jay, lives in Kansas. When she's not writing, she likes to read, work in the garden, and walk the dogs. A Hugo Award–winning illustrator, she is best known for her series *Woof: The House Dragon.* Her songs about humanity's future in space are sung at science fiction conventions throughout the world and have been recorded in cassette form: *Cosmic Concepts More Complete, Star*Song,* and *Fire Dream.* Her adult novel, *The Alien Dark,* appeared in 1990. She is the author of *Star Trek: Deep Space Nine®: Arcade,* a novel for young readers. She is working on another story about *The Secret World of Alex Mack.*

YOU COULD WIN A TRIP TO NICKELODEON STUDIOS!

1 Grand Prize: A weekend(4 day/3 night)trip to Nickelodeon Studios in Orlando, FL
3 First Prizes: A Nickelodeon collection of ten videos
25 Second Prizes: A Clarissa board game
50 Third Prizes: One year subscription to Nickelodeon Magazine

Name_____Birthdate_____

Address_____

City_____State_____Zip_____

Daytime Phone_____

POCKET BOOKS/"Win a trip to Nickelodeon Studios" SWEEPSTAKES
Sweepstakes Sponsors Official Rules:

1. No Purchase Necessary. Enter by submitting the completed Official Entry Form (no copies allowed) or by sending on a 3" x 5" card your name and address to the Pocket Books/Nickelodeon Sweepstakes, Advertising and Promotion Department, 13th Floor, 1230 Avenue of the Americas, NY, NY 10020. Entries must be received by 12/29/95. Not responsible for lost, late or misdirected mail or for typographical errors in the entry form or rules. Enter as often as you wish, but one entry per envelope. Winners will be selected at random from all entries received in a drawing to be held on or about 1/2/96.

2. Prizes: One Grand Prize: A weekend (four day/three night) trip for up to four persons (the winning minor, one parent or legal guardian and two guests) including round-trip coach airfare from the major U.S. airport nearest the winner's residence, ground transportation or car rental, meals, three nights in a hotel (one room, occupancy for four) and a tour of Nickelodeon Studios in Orlando, Florida (*approx. retail value $3500.00*), Three First Prizes: A Nickelodeon collection of ten videos (*approx. retail value $200.00 each*), Twenty-Five Second Prizes: A Clarissa board game (*approx. retail value $15.00 each*), Fifty Third Prizes: One year subscription to

Nickelodeon magazine (*approx. retail value $18.00 each*).

3. The sweepstakes is open to residents of the U.S. and Canada no older than fourteen as of 12/29/95. Proof of age required to claim prize. Prizes will be awarded to the winner's parent or legal guardian. Void in Puerto Rico and wherever else prohibited or restricted by law. Employees of Viacom International Inc., their suppliers, subsidiaries, affiliates, agencies, participating retailers, and their families living in the same household are not eligible.

4. One prize per person or household. Prizes are not transferable and may not be substituted. All prizes will be awarded. The odds of winning a prize depend upon the number of entries received.

5. If a winner is a Canadian resident, then he/she must correctly answer a skill-based question administered by mail. Any litigation respecting the conduct and awarding of a prize in this publicity contest may be submitted to the Regie des Loteries et Courses du Quebec.

6. All federal, state and local taxes are the responsibility of the winners. Winners will be notified by mail. Winners may be required to execute and return an Affidavit of Eligibility and Release and all other legal documents which the sweepstakes sponsor may require (including a W-9 tax form) within 15 days of notification or an alternate winner will be selected.

7. Winners grant Pocket Books and MTV Networks the right to use their names, likenesses, and entries for any advertising, promotion and publicity purposes without further compensation to or permission from the entrants, except where prohibited by law.

8. Winners agree that Viacom International Inc., its parent, subsidiaries and affiliated companies, or any sponsors, as well as the employees of each of these, shall have no liability in connection with the collection, acceptance or use of the prizes awarded herein.

9. By participating in this sweepstakes, entrants agree to be bound by these rules and the decisions of the judges and sweepstakes sponsors, which are final in all matters relating to the sweepstakes.

10. For a list of major prize winners, (available after 1/2/96) send a stamped, self-addressed envelope to Prize Winners, Pocket Books/Nickelodeon Sweepstakes Advertising and Promotion Department, 13th Floor, 1230 Avenue of the Americas, NY, NY 10020